DRAWING STRENGTH FROM WORDS

A Four Horsemen Novel

By

C. A. King

Cover Design: Ravenborn Covers

Editor: J.D. Cunegan

Look for other books by C.A. King, including:

The Portal Prophecies:
Book I - A Keeper's Destiny
Book II - A Halloween's Curse
Book III - Frost Bitten
Book IV - Sleeping Sands
Book V - Deadly Perceptions
Book VI - Finding Balance

Tomoiya's Story:

Book I: Escape to Darkness
Book II: Collecting Tears

Surviving the Sins:

Book I: Answering the Call
Book II: Pride

When Leaves Fall: A Different Point of View Story

Peach Coloured Daisies: A Cursed by the Gods Story

Flower Shields: A Four Horsemen Novel

Miracles Not Included

Twisted Tales of A Dead End Street

Shot Through The Heart: A Faerie Tale

Cover Design: Ravenborn Covers

First Printing: July 16, 2018

ISBN: 978-1-988301-39-6

Kings Toe Publishing
kingstoepublishing@gmail.com
Burlington, Ontario. Canada

Opening Thoughts

Creation. Over the years, there have been hundreds of plausible explanations for how and why man came into being. The problem that has plagued an entire race throughout the ages was and always will be which of these interpretations, if any, held truth.

Humans have always required knowledge. Where did they come from? Why were they put here? This whole species has searched for explanations locked somewhere in the limits of their own minds. Imagination itself held the key to opening the door. Once unlocked, the possibilities were endless. Myths and legends were born and passed down through the ages.

A simple recanting of these stories has, without question, revealed proof of a common thread between them. Few would argue that, at the root of most origin tales, there existed the acknowledgment of the presence of one or more supreme beings - someone or thing credited for having brought about all life on earth. Where these celestial beings, referred to as Gods, came from may never be known. If, however, one knew where to look, one could find evidence of their time here - or perhaps the scars they left behind.

The following was one of those stories - a love story gone wrong.

Prologue

In a place where creativity through art, dance, poetry, and music was coveted above all else, a child was born. From the very beginning, Ihenna was thought of as by far the most beautiful of her kind. In a realm mesmerized by refinement, it was of no surprise to anyone that, when she came of age to take a mate, suitors lined up with unimaginable gifts to win her hand and her heart.

It was Nakamire who won in the end. His admiration for Ihenna was unmatched. Of course, when he presented his gift, he had no idea one of his nine brothers was in the line behind him. Zahare never had the opportunity to profess his love, though it wouldn't have mattered if he did. Nothing could compare to Nakamire's creation - a world filled with beauty, born from pure love.

This new world was designed in two levels. One, in the open, where plants and animals roamed free and another below, where his bride-to-be could escape to if she became overwhelmed by her surroundings.

It was the surface Ihenna fell in love with. Enough so that she decided to make it her home. A grand castle was built, surrounded by stunning gardens filled with her favourite flowers. It was a temple for his bride-to-be that captured everything she held in high regard. Her future husband had attended to every detail, including the race of man to admire her. They showered her with beautiful words, art, and music. Her life was a dream world where only the things she loved most existed.

Being worshiped as a god had a certain undeniable appeal. Nakamire's siblings and friends quickly joined the proud couple, eager to stay in paradise and share in the abundance of happiness - albeit some relished their newfound roles a little too much. A new race of demigods was born carrying the bloodlines of both the creator and creation.

Unbeknownst to them, not everyone shared in their bliss. Every day Zahare witnessed their love, he grew more bitter, eventually taking up residence alone below the surface world. Blatant attempts to fill the growing void inside him with numerous women failed. A race of half-breeds born from jealousy and rage were his only reward.

Zahare despised this new world. His own offspring became his personal demons - twisting his consciousness further into the depths of insanity. It was there, in the lunacy of his own mind, that a plan took life. He would kill Nakamire and take Ihenna for himself.

Fueled by the words of a madman, his demons embraced the power each inherited - their only goal to be the one to sit by their father's side and win his approval.

When the day came, Zahare approached his brother, deception dancing on his lips in the form of a smile - a poisoned dagger concealed.

One prearranged distraction was all he needed to unsheathe his weapon and, with every ounce of anger he had stored, plunge it deep into flesh.

It was over in a flash, but it wasn't Nakamire who lay lifeless on the marble floor. Ihenna used her own body to block the attack. Zahare killed the only woman he had ever loved. Screams of anguish by not one, but two gods rumbled through the skies, quaking the earth.

If Zahare hadn't been consumed by madness before, he was now. Blaming not only his brother, but also the race of man and the world they lived in, he called forth his strongest demons to unleash their powers born from his rage: pestilence; famine; war; and death. Demanding total destruction, he promised to take the most loyal of his spawn to another world - one ruled by darkness.

Nakamire had lost his true love, but he wasn't about to let the world she held so dear suffer the same fate. With half-breeds by his side, a battle like no other ensued. The others, Nakamire's friends and family, once thought of as mighty gods, fled, refusing to be caught in the wake of certain destruction. They were, in fact, on the verge of being prophetic.

Heavy casualties were suffered on both sides. In the end, only one could win. Nakamire and the demigods stood victorious, but on that day, there were no feasts or celebrations.

With all he had already lost, Nakamire couldn't bear to destroy his brother as well. Instead, he sealed Zahare and as many of his brother's demon offspring as could be found beneath the surface world - a jail meant to provide a constant reminder of the atrocities that had been committed. Four locked gates stood between the two plateaus. One demigod was chosen as protector of each gate, should Zahare ever find a way to open them.

In the wake of devastation, Nakamire tried to rebuild - hoping to bask in the memory of Ihenna's happiness. Like so many others, he too turned to female companionship, attempting to fill the void. By the time he realized his mistake, he had already become a father many times over. Unlike the other gods, however, he felt a connection to these demigods. Torn between an inability to remain in mourning and his love for his children, Nakamire was forced to make a choice. With heavy heart he left his creation, allowing only those born of his world to return with him. Zahare, the demons, and the demigods were all left behind. That day the gate to the heavens was destroyed, never to open again.

*****

Over time, truths became legends - merely tales passed down from generation to generation. Slowly, the facts mutated - a little sensationalism added at a time until only a thread of authenticity remained.

Demigods and demons alike disappeared. Records of their existence were destroyed. What once was, became little more than the whispers of secret organizations. They, however, weren't gone, but were merely lying in wait, to one day appear again.

The guardians of the four gates remained faithful to their cause through the ages - seeking out and destroying demons trying to free their forefather from the confines of the hell he had been sentenced to live in.

Thousands of years later, a new threat appeared on the horizon...

Chapter One

Dust took flight, dislodged by the force of a wooden gavel slamming down on its circular base. Tiny white particles, barely visible to the eye, floated down in no hurry to return to the spots from whence they came. They were in Lady Justice's house, and while she might have worn a blindfold, those in her employ most certainly did not. Here, even the smallest particle of dirt had reason to be petrified by the wrath of the presiding judge.

A second loud bang sounded, echoing through the courtroom. This one powerful enough to send vibrations up and down Ryder's spine. If there had been any doubt the judge's decision was final, it was long gone - frightened off by the strong grasp of right hand of the law.

Guilty. That word had a permanent place in his mind and, with this latest loss, was etched on his soul. That was to be expected though. He had, after all, heard it enough times. This was his tenth conviction and every one for a crime he hadn't committed.

Ryder swallowed, feeling the tie around his neck tightening with all the care of a noose's grip. He loosened its hold, sticking two fingers inside his collar, hoping to stretch it enough to allow some breathing room. Suits simply weren't comfortable. He had no idea how businessmen made it through one day after another locked in the designer jail known as high fashion.

The prosecutor, to Ryder's right, looked down at his paperwork, nodding and moving sheets around as if pondering different options. Given a chance, he had an arsenal of ploys tucked away up his sleeve and his latest bout of showboating was only just the beginning. It took years of appearances before numerous judges to perfect his performance, but perfected it was. All the little man had to do was appear to know what the best route to follow was. Once that was accomplished, it was easier to convince others to agree with his proposals.

As an opposing attorney, he was as stereotypical as they came - a book lying open at the same place, never once having its pages flipped. If he had been part of a dictionary, he would be listed under P for pathetic. At least, that would have been the perfect place for a picture of the shell of a man to appear. The twinkle in his eye that had once represented all the great feats a young enthusiastic counselor planned to accomplish was all but extinguished - making way for mediocrity and complacency.

Generic enough to represent the masses, he was the epitome of a middle-aged, balding man who owned only one suit, and by the looks of his shirt, didn't own an iron or perhaps didn't know how to use one. From the way one of his hands clung to a wedding ring, his pudgy fingers twisting it, there was little doubt his wife had recently left him - most likely for a colleague with a fatter pension.

Holding a position of prestige meant nothing if it didn't come part and parcel with the benefits that usually accompanied such titles. Practitioners employed within the system itself simply didn't make the same income as those who represented individuals with fat wallets and money to burn.

Every ounce of loathing he had for his own miserable existence, every moment of regret for not making it further in his career, was about to come pouring out through his dull grey eyes. The second it escaped, all that pent-up anger would be redirected at the easiest target in the room.

Being the scapegoat wasn't anything new to Ryder. He'd been blamed all his life for everything that was wrong with anyone else's. If the court had its way, he would be sentenced to burn in hell for every little detail that was wrong in each and every one of their lives. Why no one else could see that as clearly as he did was a mystery.

The only thing standing between another grave injustice and even swifter punishment was Merv.

Ryder side-eyed his own representation - the same man who always managed to come to his aid no matter what the situation. His attorney didn't even flinch, all the while knowing he was being watched. Being scrutinized under a microscope came with the territory of counsel for the defence.

As far as lawyers went, Merv didn't miss a step. Confidence oozed from his pores, forcing those who opposed him to take a few steps back and rethink their plans. He possessed a rare talent: the gift of the gab, having been born with a silver tongue that could cast doubt on a nun's testimony about the existence of God. The only thing that didn't make sense was what a professional of his caliber was doing defending a petty criminal up on vandalism charges.

The prosecutor cleared his throat. "Your honour," he said, voice wavering slightly. "If I may, I'd like to offer a few suggestions for sentencing."

"I think our honourable judge is capable of deciding a fitting punishment on his own," Merv argued.

"This particular offender has been in front of this court on numerous occasions. Clearly, stiffer penalties are needed. I recommend placement in a psychiatric detention facility for evaluation." The prosecutor dropped his papers, granting his full attention to the judge. One hand behind his back twitched, a primitive form of sign language based purely on fear.

"Your honour," Merv started, "there is a waiting list of criminals truly needing such a placement. Clearly, a simple case of vandalism isn't a priority."

The gavel slammed down on the wooden desk again. "Order!" the judge bellowed. "I won't have this court turned into a circus. As it stands, I agree with both of you. The psychiatric evaluation centre has better use for its limited spaces. At the same time, this young man is a multiple-time offender. Jail time simply isn't working."

The judge pushed a tiny pair of round glasses further up the bridge of his nose as he scribbled notes on the back of court documents in a form only he himself would later be able to decipher. "That is why this court orders a term of community service."

"Your honour," the prosecutor objected, pulling a handkerchief from one pocket to daub spots of perspiration forming on his brow. "Such a lenient sentence is a crime in itself. I beg the court to reconsider."

"Silence!" the judge demanded, pointing his gavel at the lawyer, suggesting that lack of compliance might result in the bald spot on his head being the next place it came down. "The ancient history library is going through major renovations. They could use some... volunteer help. I expect the term to be served in full there. There are adequate accommodations located on the premises. The defendant is to remain a guest there for a period of one year."

"Thank you, your honour," Merv said.

"Make no mistake, sir," the judge stated, "if your client fails to perform his duties, I will revise my judgement to accept the prosecution's suggestions. Are we clear?"

"Yes, sir," Ryder replied. He stood perfectly still, a statue frozen in time, waiting for the judge to make a swift exit before breathing.

The worst was over and yet only now beads of sweat were making their presence known. A familiar feeling loomed over him. He didn't even need to turn around to actually see it to know it existed. The heat radiating across his back simply wasn't natural. Some would have called it paranoia. He, however, knew it was from being watched, and if he had to guess, whoever it was, had the eyes of a dead man.

Fingers rubbed over his face, as if scrubbing away dried-on dirt. Inside Ryder trembled, but on the exterior, he had no intention of showing fear. The bodies and faces connected to those glares often changed, but the black of their eyes always remained the same. They followed him everywhere he went and had since he was just a boy.

Never underestimate the power of a stare. The fright it instilled alone was dominant, but that wasn't where its power ended. That lifeless glare had the ability to drill deep inside him and harvest every ounce of emotion it produced. As hard as he tried to hide it all well within his core, in the end, it didn't matter. This was an opponent that had his number. At any time, the game could have ended. He was no match for them, yet they never took the final move.

Ryder's eyes glanced over at the prosecutor, who was faring no better than himself. The man slouched back in his chair, listless, save for the shaking of one knee, well hidden under the protection of a wooden table. The colour of his face drained to match the same shade of white as the papers scattered in front of him.

The weight of a thousand souls sentenced to purgatory lifted off of Ryder's shoulders in search of a new unfortunate victim to latch onto. The defeated lump of a lawyer was an easy target. Plain and simple, the man had failed. His penance for that failure was an endless depth of sorrow and pain brought on by the owners of those black eyes.

New shivers ran up and down Ryder's spine, these ones not knowing which way to head for safety. How many times had those bottomless pools of darkness sized him up from behind in the same manner they now did for the prosecutor?

"Ready?" Merv asked.

"Yeah," Ryder replied, still focused on the other man. "Is he okay? Maybe we should call someone."

Merv glanced over. "He's fine," he answered, ushering his client by the arm out a side door. "Losing cases is never easy."

Chapter Two

Taking a side door outside landed them in the same place as the front would have - descending the white, stone stairs in the front of the building. Ryder's long legs took two steps at a time, leaving him waiting at the bottom for his lawyer to catch up.

"A library," Ryder complained, lighting a cigarette. "What am I supposed to do in a library?" He inhaled deeply, catching sight of a couple on the opposite side of the street. *Those eyes.*

"You could try reading, for one," Merv replied. He stopped short, turning to his client. "This isn't optional. Time will fly by. You'll see. You need to go there and just do a good job."

"Like my life depends on it?" Ryder scoffed, flicking the ashes off the stick wedged firmly between two fingers.

"It just might," Merv replied, grabbing his client's cigarette and tossing it on the ground. The sole of his shoe came down hard, extinguishing it. "I won't always be able to win for you. That ever-growing rap sheet of yours is going to be your downfall. One day, it won't matter what I say."

"Why not give up on me, then?" Ryder snapped.

Merv pushed him up against the black car sent to fetch them. "I made a promise and I intend to do everything I can to keep it. A little help from you would be nice once in a while."

"I didn't do anything," Ryder blurted out.

"Funny thing is, you never do," Merv complained. "If it truly is the people around you who always get you in trouble, you need to find new friends. Stop letting them drag you down. Don't take the fall all the time. They aren't your responsibility."

"Easy for you to say," Ryder replied, fixing his collar. "It seems everyone is out to get me... except you."

"Then don't bite the hand that feeds you!" Merv exclaimed, opening the car door. "Get in. I'm taking you to get settled. I'll arrange for your possessions to be brought over later. Use your time at the library to rethink things. Your parents would have wanted you to do better for yourself. I want you to do better for yourself."

"Dad!" a girl exclaimed, running towards them - no more than fifteen, but trying to look thirty. A strong breeze caught her skirt, lifting it high enough to satisfy the needs of any peeping toms hanging out in front of the courthouse waiting for their cases to be heard.

Merv groaned, rolling his eyes. "Darling," he said, turning to face his daughter. "What are you doing here?"

"Do I need a reason to visit my father?" she cooed. "I saw on the calendar you were in court this morning and thought we could grab some lunch."

Merv chuckled. "I'd love nothing more, but I am a little busy." He motioned to Ryder already seated in the car. "Let's cut to the chase. Why are you really here, Mirabelle?"

Mirabelle shrugged her shoulders, her arms flailing up high, before falling back down at her sides. Trading in her pleasant school-girl smile for a dissatisfied pout, she linked her arm with her father's. "Mother isn't being fair."

"Oh, Mirabelle," Merv complained. "Is this about the grounding again? We have been over this already. Your mother's decision is final. I am not going to go behind her back and change things. You need to work this out with her."

Mirabelle stomped her foot. "How can you agree with her? It's totally unfair. Everyone is going to the party Saturday. I'll be the laughing stock of town if I don't go."

"Mirabelle!" Merv yelled, his hand reaching into one pocket to retrieve a brown leather wallet. A crisp bill snapped between his first two fingers and thumb. "Take a cab straight home," he ordered, handing her the money. "We'll discuss this later."

"But..."

Merv waggled a finger in her direction. "No buts," he said. "If your mother finds out about this, you could find yourself missing a lot more than just one party. I have to go back to work now. I trust you have the sense to listen to reason."

Mirabelle's shoe kicked at the array of cigarette butts scattered over the sidewalk: her eyes locked on the ground. "I suppose," she muttered. "It's not fair, though,"

Merv bent over, planting his lips on her cheek with a peck. "Tell your mom I'll be late for dinner."

Chapter Three

Mirabelle watched the car speed away, leaving her standing at the side of the road, hands planted firmly on her hips. What father did that? She was facing the biggest disaster of her life. Was it too much to ask that he be there for her?

Life simply wasn't fair. She'd spent months dreaming about having even an inkling of a chance of going out with Bobby - a dream every girl at her school shared. None of them, however, had the same connection she did with him.

The other girls only saw him as an object; the most popular guy in school; the quarterback of the football team; and a stepping stone to the best social life anyone could ever want. They were all far too shallow. Bobby deserved better. He deserved to be with her. What she had with Bobby was truly spiritual.

A moment of contentment filled with sunny skies and rainbows transformed into a fast moving wave of grey clouds fuelled by anger. Her parents were ruining everything. What if she never had the chance to bring their love to its full fruition?

Her own sense of self-importance trumped paying attention to her surroundings. Her feet tangled over a brown leather briefcase sticking out from under a bench. With a fall already underway, she clenched her eyes closed, waiting for the inevitable. If she ended up with bruises, her father was to blame. Then at least she could have proven child abuse.

While it was true time slowed when one fell, the amount that passed by in this case was a little too long. Her eyes blinked open, their gaze returned by a set almost equally as beautiful as her own.

"Are you okay?" the man asked, returning her to her feet in a swooping motion. "That could have been a nasty tumble. I should be more careful where I put my bag. I accept all responsibility. Please accept my humble apology." He bowed his head to her.

A silver grey suit; salt and pepper hair and a smile that could melt the heart of an ice queen - this man truly was her knight in shining armour and she the damsel... no, princess in distress willing to be saved. The lines around his eyes smiled at her, agreeing with her assessment. A simple wink sent her heart fluttering in directions she hadn't known possible.

What a fool she had been to think she could feel love for any boy at her school. His name had already been banished from her lips, forever lost to her tongue. Girls matured at a much faster rate. An older man was what she needed and exactly what she'd just found. This was true love.

"It was completely my fault," she replied, batting her eyelashes. "I should pay more attention to where I walk. I'm Mirabelle."

"A pleasure," he said, taking her hand. He brushed his lips against the back. "Allow me to introduce myself. I am Dante."

"Dante," she echoed, memorized without magic. In her daze, everything became clear. Mirabelle flipped her bleach-blonde hair, which according to her was completely natural. The roots peeking out every time the wind blew screamed otherwise, demanding a bleach touch-up in the coming days.

"Are you in a hurry?" Dante asked. "It would be my pleasure to buy you lunch for your troubles. Perhaps you can share with me what it is preoccupying your pretty little head."

"You want to listen to me?" Mirabelle asked, biting her bottom lip. "You aren't too busy?"

"Don't be silly," Dante answered. "A princess such as yourself deserves everyone's full attention."

Mirabelle giggled. Somewhere hidden in the high-pitched awkwardness lurked a budding flirtatious woman. This was her coming-out party. Her dress swayed back and forth with her turning body, feet planted in one spot. Her youth was attractive. Not only did she know it, she had every intention of working it.

"Dante," a woman called out.

Mirabelle's playful grin turned south. Glancing over the competition brought a scowl to her face, aging her drastically. The thought that her perfect man might already have another woman hadn't crossed her mind until that moment. This one, however, didn't appear to have the natural beauty required to be of any concern.

"Amy," Dante replied, taking the woman's arm and pulling her to the side. "I didn't expect to see you here. What can I do for you?"

"I did what you asked," Amy replied, scratching her head. A piece of hair bulged out of a messy ponytail, pulled back without a brush. Her lips quivered, frightened of the words they were about to form.

Mirabelle cleared her throat, smiling apologetically. "A tickle," she explained, shrugging her shoulders. "That lunch did come with a drink, I hope."

"Of course," Dante replied, the dashing smile of her precious knight returning. "Where are my manners? Mirabelle, this is Amy. She's a... client of mine. I hope you don't mind if we drop her off at home on our way."

"Taking care of business should always come first," Mirabelle answered, linking her arm with his free one.

"My sentiments exactly," Dante agreed, taking the lead to his awaiting car and driver.

Chapter Four

Gabrielle glanced from side to side. This wasn't right. She had made the same trip several times before without ever having an issue. The closest public building to the location she wanted to go was always the destination. The library should have been included in the definition of public building. So why was she outside the courthouse?

She shrugged her shoulders. There didn't seem to be an explanation. When dealing with magic, there didn't always need to be a reason. One simply had to trust the powers that be knew what they were doing. Faith wasn't typically one of her family's strong suits, but everyone had to have at least a little to survive in any world.

She hesitated after taking each step down, dawdling with purpose. If this was planned and there was something she was meant to see, she didn't want to miss it. Unfortunately, there wasn't one thing that seemed out of the ordinary. She inhaled deeply, searching for the scent of demons nearby but coming up empty. Instead she found something just as putrid.

The burning in her lungs took a few minutes to pass. Safely inside the personal fortress she called home, every breath was pure and clean - the way things were meant to be. Perhaps that was why she didn't ever want to leave; each time she did, the world seemed to have taken a turn for the worse, becoming a little more polluted and a lot less enjoyable. She cleared her throat, one hand grasping the collar of her trench coat tight around her neck.

The atmosphere of this world had changed in more than one way. It wasn't just busier, it was fuller. Insignificant wasn't a feeling she was used to. The shoulders of strangers passing by banged into her own without an ounce of remorse. Here on the street, she was merely a hindrance: a blockade in someone's way. That was exactly how these mortals treated her, not one worried about who she was or what she might be capable of.

The weight of stares from nameless faces passing by chopped away at her. Inch by inch she shrunk, wondering how long it would be before she disappeared altogether. That would have been too easy, especially for a demigod.

In her life, everything and anything was a test, and this was one she planned to pass with flying colours. With straightened posture, she took charge of her person, working the strut of a supermodel.

Being gawked at wasn't anything new. This world had never truly accepted her from day one. There had always been emphasis on male superiority. Throughout the ages she'd seen it: lived it - a common thread that bound one generation to another. Things might have seemed to improve, but in reality it was only a lone drop in the bucket on a hot summer's day. Life itself would perish if it had to rely on that.

This new world, with all its technological improvements and advancements, was no different than days of old. There comes a time when a person grows tired of being disappointed with what everyone else calls progressive changes. Mankind was never going to be able to accept a woman in the role of one of the four horsemen. That, however, wasn't what all the giggles and whispers going on around her were about.

Whoever said styles came back was a liar. Sitting in her private library might have been good for research, but not for fashion sense. Keeping her nose in a book was so much easier than fitting in with society. Books she was good with; people... not so much. The ones surrounding her now had enough snickers and sly comments to reinforce her dislike for social interactions.

Her pace quickened. There were still a few blocks to go before she could alter her look without garnering more attention than she already had. Perhaps her brothers knew what they were talking about. Installing a connection in their home to the outside world for gathering information didn't seem so bad from where she now stood.

Gabby pulled down her sunglasses, a present from her brother Uri. They had been all the rage that year, although she couldn't remember exactly what year it had been. To her it seemed like only the day before when she opened the box. A hyena couldn't have laughed harder at the sight of the round oversized goggles. Still, she had tried them on, along with the multi-coloured silk scarf that currently covered her head.

Very few people had pure white hair. Hiding it at times had always proved a difficult task; at least, that had been her excuse for not venturing out of their homestead for a few decades. She had always stood out like a sore thumb, even on a good day. Now, her attempts to disguise her normal appearance had become the problem.

Brothers! They always tried to come up with a way around any blockade she threw up.

"Brothers," she mumbled. That was the answer. Her hand dove into her pocket, searching for the phone Michael had insisted she bring along. Her arm jolted, a sharp pain running through her fingertips. Adrenaline pumped through her veins as pain mutated into an uncomfortable tickle. It wasn't until only a tingling sensation remained that she realized what had happened. Electricity wasn't her friend.

She glanced down at the phone lying innocently in the palm of her hand. It was hard to believe such a small device packed such a viscous punch. She had a brand new reason to hate technology. One finger reached out. There was no legitimate reason for fear of a second shock, but her finger wasn't convinced. It shook, unsure of what contact would bring.

The button went in. Nothing happened. A scowl crossed her face as her finger pressed down on it again - this time with purpose. The screen remained blank. Her fingers closed around it, knuckles whitening.

"Why won't you work?!" she yelled, shaking it up and down. The screen remained blank, mocking her feeble attempts.

"Are you alright?" A man asked.

Gabby smiled. "This phone..."

"Let me guess," the man interrupted. "A loaner?"

"Exactly," Gabby replied, pursing her lips together with a slight upward curl. "I can't even seem to turn it on."

"Let me see," the man offered. "Well, there is your problem. The battery is dead. It's happened to me before. You take in your trusted companion for fixing and they give you an out-of-date model to use with only a few minutes' worth of charge on it. You'll need to give it a full night plugged in to get it back to where it should be."

"Right," Gabby replied, biting her lip. "How silly if me... I'll do that. Thank you."

"Did you need to borrow mine?"

"No," Gabby blurted out. "I was only..."

"Checking for messages?" the man said. "I get it. These things are attached to us. It's crazy. Good luck."

"Bye." She watched the gentleman walk away. His generous offer might have come in handy, if it weren't for the fact all the numbers she needed to call were programmed into the device that wouldn't turn on.

She let out a huff. Michael said to take a phone. There was no mention of a cord to plug it in with. The phone vanished into her pocket, rendered useless. For now, she was on her own.

Chapter Five

Ryder glanced up at the white steps, accentuated by old-fashioned columns. The whole building's architecture was from a style long forgotten - one that now only belonged in depictions of ancient times and definitely not leading to a modern-day library entrance. The similarities between the path before him and the one he'd just left behind at the courthouse was daunting. Whoever designed one had his hand in the creation of the other.

He shook his head. None of that mattered in the greater scheme of things. Taking the steps two at a time, he left his lawyer bringing up the rear for the second occasion that day. Merv always had his back before. Why should that be any different here?

Ryder paused at the entrance. Years had passed since he had been there - the last time was shortly before the accident that claimed the lives of his parents. A layer of moisture formed on his brow, not quite wet enough to be called sweat. It wasn't perspiration, either. That word was reserved for the middle and upper class, a group he wasn't a member of.

Heat wasn't the problem. A straightforward test using the back of his hand confirmed his skin was cool. That simple touch became a catalyst to a much larger problem. The same dampness spreading like a virus, making its presence known on the palms of both of his hands.

Worry. It did nothing but waste the head start he'd accumulated. Ryder pushed forward. The tips of his fingers on one hand almost reached the handle. Instead, the door swung open. He barely had time to blink before receiving an up-close and personal view of the door. A rare moment of awkwardness ensued, his arms flailing. The impact caught him off-guard, his nose taking the brunt of the pressure. It wasn't broken, but there'd be bruising in the coming hours, and without any ice to keep the swelling at bay, it wasn't going to be pretty.

He glanced up at the elderly woman exiting the building, shaking her head as she stepped over his sprawled out legs. He was on the ground injured and she was upset. That pretty much summed up how everything in his life went.

"Are you kidding me?" he snarled, fingers desperately feeling around, trying to assess the damage only a reflection could show. "An apology would be nice."

Merv shook his head. "Leave it be!" he ordered, offering a hand up. "Arguing with women never works out in any man's favour. You are on thin ice as it is. It is going to take a bit of restraint or your part to ensure you do not fall through." He pulled open the door and motioned for his companion to enter first. "Let's take a look at your new home."

"Temporary home," Ryder mumbled, his voice lowered to a whisper. Even that was too much for a library.

A tidal wave of emotions came crashing down as Ryder stepped through the door. He held his breath, knowing this was the one place he couldn't scream for help. That much had been bred into him - installed like a virus, waiting to kick in at the opportune moment and render him useless. His jaw dropped. He stood frozen - a complete system reboot needed. Luckily, Merv slapped him on the back, pushing all the right buttons.

"It's not so bad," Merv said. "You can catch up on some light reading while you are here." The lawyer laughed, paying no attention to the occupants of the room, scrutinizing his actions.

"Reading," Ryder echoed, "great."

Reading wasn't high on his list of priorities. There had been a time when listening to his mother's voice reciting poems and stories had been the highlight of his days. They were all but memories now - ones that were fading fast, leaving behind a scar that prevented him from seeking out books for his own enjoyment. The judge hit his gavel on the proverbial nail in choosing this sentencing. A library was far worse than any jail could have ever been.

"This is Daniel," Merv stated. "He'll be showing you around after the library closes." A tug on a gold chain popped a pocket watch into the palm of his hand. A flip of the thumb was all it took to expose its shiny dial. "I have to be going. Your things should be arriving soon. Remember, keep your head down and nose clean. It's best if you remain within these walls. Meals will be provided to you. If you need me, call." He waved his hand and was out the door before Ryder had a chance to say a word.

Ryder arched his eyebrows. "Hi, Daniel," he said, offering his hand to shake.

Daniel alternated his glance between Ryder's face and hand. He shook his head, returning his attention solely to the papers on the desk in front of him. "Have a seat," he ordered in a low tone. "We'll be closing soon." Hospitality simply wasn't in the books.

Chapter Six

Dante kept his gaze focused on the two girls riding with him. His private limousine was fully stocked, offering an array of drinks; types of tobacco; and sweet delicacies - yet neither requested a single thing.

For one, that behaviour was completely understandable. Amy wanted nothing other than a good fix of drugs to numb away the pitiful life she led.

Such a waste! A young girl, barely twenty, and utterly spent. There were plenty of women twice her age who had more left in the tank. He could almost feel the vibrations of her shaking knee from the opposite seat. Other than that motion, Amy kept to herself, only moving her hand to and from her mouth in order to examine what was left of her nails after biting them.

Mirabelle, on the other hand, was a conundrum. She sat posture perfect and completely attentive. As a girl who obviously insisted on the finer things in life, she should have been relishing in every morsel located only fingertips away. He would have to wait to figure out the answer to her until after his business with Amy was concluded, but figure her out, he would.

Signs of worry crept over his muse's face as their ride came to a stop. This wasn't the type of neighbourhood a fancy car parked in - at least for very long. The road itself was a graveyard for vehicles which had made that very mistake - now unable to move; missing parts; and covered in graffiti.

A shadow hovered overhead, no doubt made entirely from evaporated tears - a result of the misfortune that had fallen upon the inhabitants of the low-income housing project. They were society's throwaways; the ones the rest of the world turned its back on in hopes of forgetting. Poor wasn't a strong enough word to describe them. It was much more than that. These were the truly lost, both desperate and desolate.

Dante's lips turned upwards, forming an evil grin. "Right, then," he said, opening the car door. "I believe this is your stop, Amy. I'll walk you to your door. Mirabelle, do be so good as to stay inside the limo." He didn't wait for a response.

Allowing Amy to lead the way, he tipped his hat at everyone they passed. Here, he relied on his reputation to keep him safe. In most cases, it did just that. Everyone knew at least one of the rumours swirling around about Dante's power and very few were crazy enough to try to test them. Here, he was considered a god.

In reality, the seemingly misplaced worship of the masses wasn't that inappropriate. Dante was, after all, a demigod. Even if no one from this neighbourhood actually knew the truth, the way he carried himself spoke volumes.

Amy's fingers shook, keys jingling, but the correct one not finding its way into the hole to unlock the bolt. A light shone down on the door to her lower-level apartment. Remaining in plain sight wasn't something even Dante was willing to do for too long. There was an uncertainty that lent its hand to those who had nothing left to lose. They were dangerous and unpredictable at best.

Dante watched her, his foot tapping a little louder with every passing moment. There was only so much he could handle of a junkie requiring a fix in order to continue functioning. Another few hours and she'd be a useless blob, begging for anything to make her feel better and not caring what it was or how she got it. Her blatant disregard for the precious life she'd been given was, in his eyes, more than enough to justify what he was about to do.

The door creaked open. They were barely inside before Amy began a song and dance, expecting a prize to be awarded to her for the performance once it was completed.

"Can I have it now?" Amy begged, biting what was left of one of her fingernails until it bled. She pursed her lips together, scratching her head. "I really need it. I did what you asked. Please." She rolled up her sleeves in anticipation, leaving old scars and bruises that lacked the opportunity to fade visible.

"And yet, I still don't have Ryder in my possession," Dante stated. "That was the overall plan." A single finger ran across the top of a table; the only furniture worth mentioning in the room other than a mattress lying sheet-less on the floor. He blew the accumulated dust off his fingertip.

Amy shifted her weight between her two legs, a motor ready to be revved at a moment's notice. "You can't blame me for what that lawyer didn't do. I did my part. I want what's coming to me. It's only fair."

"I suppose that's true," Dante agreed. He held out a gloved fist, opening it slowly to expose several syringes. "Are these what you want? All filled and ready to use..."

Amy stumbled forward, transforming into nothing more than a ravenous beast grabbing at the first food it had seen in days. Once in her possession, she scurried away to a corner, the first needle already inserted into a vein in her arm. It was one of the last ones left that didn't collapse in fright from the mere sight of a needle.

She slid down into a heap on the floor enjoying the last buzz she'd ever feel. It was all over before Dante stepped foot outside the door.

"Your services are no longer needed," Dante snickered. He dialed emergency on Amy's phone. "I'd like to report a death." The phone landed in the room with a thud, still connected to dispatch. He pulled the door closed and headed back to his waiting ride.

"Mirabelle," he said. "What would you like for lunch?"

"Something fancy," Mirabelle answered, doom and gloom instantly transforming into delight. "I'd like to go somewhere I haven't been before... somewhere exotic." She reached for a bottle of champagne, pouring two glasses.

Dante flashed a toothy smile and a wink. Whatever had held her back earlier was completely gone now. There was an air about her demeanor, one he had seen many a time before. This girl could have easily been mistaken for having the soul of a demon, even if she wasn't directly related to one. She would no doubt make him a more than worthy foot soldier; one he planned to put to good use immediately.

"After we eat, I'd like to introduce you to a few friends," Dante suggested. "I think you'll find our cause most interesting. You may even decide to join us."

"I'd be happy to join," Mirabelle blurted out. "As long as I am by your side, I know it's the right thing to do."

"Perfect!" Dante said. "To making new friends." He held his glass in the air. The two clanged together sealing the deal.

Chapter Seven

Gabrielle ducked into the closest establishment she could find: a tavern. It wasn't ideal to drink in the afternoon, but it would have to do. She needed to ditch her unnecessary extra layers of clothing and this was the most inconspicuous way available.

"Afternoon," a man behind the bar said. "If you are going for the mysterious look... that might be a bit overkill."

"I guess you are right," Gabby replied, removing the sunglasses and scarf. She slung her tan trench coat over the back of a bar stool, taking the seat beside it.

"What can I get you?" he asked, using a wink as punctuation for his words.

"A coffee, black," she replied, her long white hair swinging back and forth, restricted only by a tight elastic at the back.

"Imagine that. A pretty lady like you, coming to a place like this for a coffee," a man said from a table in the middle of the room.

"That's Earl," the barkeep said, placing a cup of steaming java in front of Gabby. "I'm Ted."

"Let ole Earl buy you a real drink," the man demanded, strolling over. The smell of whiskey mixed with tobacco wafted off his words.

"Thank you for the offer, but I'm fine with the coffee," Gabby replied. She lifted the cup to her lips and blew gently before taking the first sip.

"You know, I think the misses is a lightweight," Earl boasted to his crew. "I bet she can't handle a single shot, not like a man could anyways."

A fire kindled in Gabby's eyes. Proving herself was something she had done her entire life. One more time was just another drop in the bucket. "You paying?" she muttered over top of the mug.

"That's what I wanted to hear," Earl stated, glancing her up and down. His hands smacked together, rubbing between them the beginnings of a plan. His perverted mind provided all the necessary details, complete with intricate steps showing exactly what he wanted to do to her after and putting it on display.

Earl was the worst sort of man. Gabby knew everything about him. The original prototype she'd fought against for centuries. He was a beast with no morals, and even worse, he wasn't afraid to let it show. Of course, the whole scheme hinged on one thing. He needed her too drunk to be able to walk or put up a fight.

Men! They always underestimated her. She could drink all three of her brothers under the table. One pathetic mortal man wasn't going to be a problem. She wanted... no, she needed to put Earl in his place just like she had every other male naysayer she'd met before.

"Line 'em up, Ted!" Earl demanded, tapping his fingers on the bar surface.

Ted placed a series of six shot glasses in front of them both. Without waiting for the last to be poured, Earl finished his first. His fist slammed down, almost sending waves of the precious liquid over the edges of those untouched. "Woo-wee! That's a fine drink! Your turn, little lady."

Gabby grasped one of the small glasses set out before her. Tossing her head back, she threw the clear liquid contents down her throat without hesitation. The tingling burn of the first taste brought back memories of hard-fought wars and the long victory parties following them. One local tavern or another was forced to put up with their antics for an entire evening. They were no different than the one she now sat in. The bitter sweet taste of a battle deservedly won and the pain of needless deaths still seemed to linger on her lips. All it took was a single tang on the tip of her tongue to bring back the sensations of the past - ones she desperately wanted to forget.

Dante!

She hadn't considered the possibility of running into him the same way Michael had.

"Bottoms up," Earl said, lifting his final shot in the air.

Gabby followed suit, tossing back her remaining five. "We can call it even right now," she offered.

Earl pursed his lips together and threw down another wad of bills. "Fill 'em up again, Ted."

"You sure, Earl?" Ted asked, arching his brow.

"Since when you did you care where the money came from?" Earl blurted out. "I'm paying. You pour!"

Gabby shook her head. The shots passed by her lips with ease - the burning sensations now gone, numbed away by alcohol. Her throat was the only part of her affected.

"Again!" Earl yelled, desperation reflecting in his eyes. He'd invested too much money to give up now. A hooker would have cost him less.

"Can I have a larger glass?" Gabby asked. She poured all six shots in when it arrived, swallowing the lot in one go.

Earl's jaw dropped open. He staggered backwards, two friends catching him before a nasty fall.

"What are you?" he slurred. "Some kind of devil in disguise? No woman can drink like that and feel nothing."

"I'm no demon," Gabby replied. "You, sir, underestimate the strength we females can have."

"Oh," Earl slurred, pointing his glass, the contents spilling over the sides. "You're one of those activists. A Femninastic..."

"Get him outta here, boys," Ted demanded. "He needs to sleep it off. Next time he wants to take a woman home, I suggest he ask instead of trying to outdrink her."

A warm laughter filled the room, easing the mood.

"Thanks," Gabby said, going back to her coffee. "Sorry about your friend. I have a competitive streak that I find hard to keep under control sometimes."

"Earl isn't my friend," Ted explained, wiping down spills and splashes. "He is just another regular. Paying customers keep this place open."

Gabby nodded to a television in the corner. "Would you mind turning up the volume?"

"Sure thing," Ted replied. "Looks like another murder." He shook his head. "The world isn't a safe place any more."

"It never was," Gabrielle mumbled.

"You have to admit, killing the head prosecutor is a bold move," Ted said. "Especially right after court. Someone must not have liked their verdict today. My guess: they couldn't get to the judge, so they settled for the next best thing."

"Court," Gabrielle mumbled. The coffee cup dropped from her hand. "Where is that?"

"Marvin Street. A block away from the library," Ted answered. "Are you okay?"

"I'm fine," Gabby replied, tossing more than enough money on the counter to cover the coffee and the cup.

There was no time to waste. The background of the footage had all the information she needed. If the black eyes of a demon were at the scene, that was where she was headed.

This murder was no accident. It was time to put the few pieces she had already collected together and look for the others that were still missing. It wouldn't take long now for a full picture to start coming together.

Chapter Eight

Daniel wasn't a man of many words. In fact, he hadn't bothered saying more than two or three from the time they met - an occupational hazard perhaps. Ryder expected a full tour and explanation of his duties after closing. What he got was a swift kick down some stairs to figure out the mock dungeon on his own.

"Categorize the books," Daniel mumbled before locking the only exit behind him.

There was no time like the present to check out his new home, starting with the hallway he'd been dropped into - sacks of potatoes were handled with more care.

Whichever interior designer came up with the dingy cave-like atmosphere must have had felines in mind. They, no doubt, would have enjoyed chasing around rodents and bugs in the dark. Unfortunately, his eyesight didn't adjust to the dimly-lit basement as well as a cat's would have.

"Of course!" Laughter escaped his throat. There was nothing like having a good chuckle at one's own misfortune and there was enough of that to keep him in hysterics for hours.

Iron brackets mounted to the wall, still intact, were irony at its best. Their sole purpose had once been to house candles. They might have even been the perfect solution to his problems: if it weren't for the fact they lacked one important thing... the wax.

He reached up and tapped a single light bulb dangling from a string. It swayed back and forth. Shadows obeyed its commands, moving rhythmically in time with its motion.

Ryder sighed. The only things missing from the doom and gloom of an eighteenth-century torture chamber were iron bars and perhaps a few torture racks. Of course, he hadn't seen the whole place yet. There was still the possibility he'd find all that and more.

The musty smell intensified the further in he travelled. *Mold! That was healthy!* Water, however, didn't appear to be the culprit. Although ruling out that possibility completely wasn't entirely in the equation. A leak in any of the rooms he passed could have been to blame for the odour. Not being able to see any outright signs of it didn't mean it wasn't there.

What he could see were books. There definitely wasn't a shortage of those. Found in every single room he glanced in, they cluttered the floors, piled in stack after stack. There were probably more books in number than grey bricks in the walls - not that he planned on counting each to prove that theory.

There were only two doors left to check. The first piqued his interest. He stepped inside, pulling a bottle from one of the wooden racks that framed the room. His lips puckered, blowing gently onto the green glass. Dust flew off, searching for a new home to layer on.

Long ago, the cellar had been used as natural refrigeration for what at the time were most likely exquisite vintages. What was left, however, was not fit for drinking. The once-vibrant wine had been left to rot, forgotten along with old texts. What remained was heavy in sediments and probably tasted of pure vinegar. A shiver ran down his spine, forcing his shoulders to shudder. The thought of ingesting the vile liquid was as frightening as the surroundings it had been abandoned in. Without a miracle, drinking such a liquid was not something worth taking a chance on.

That left only one room unchecked. Hopefully, it turned out to be some form of living quarters; otherwise, he was in trouble. Books didn't make the comfiest of beds and he wasn't about to share the cement floor with rats and bugs.

Thankfully, Ryder had never been allergic to dust, otherwise he would have spent the entire time there sneezing and wheezing. Trying not to disrupt its layers as he moved was challenging, to say the least. There was no short supply of it. Even a large cobweb blocking his path wasn't immune, its once-white silk turned grey. A few broken strands dangled down.

Ryder's eyes skimmed over the surface, searching for newer bits of silk. If this was still someone's home, he didn't want to anger its owner - at least not using his exposed skin. He shivered, goosebumps on his arms agreeing that creepy crawly spiders weren't welcome there.

Webs latched on to every nook and cranny of the basement, but this particular one hindered his arrival at the final destination. Breath held, he reached up, swatting away the tangle of tiny threads.

"Yuck!" Ryder grimaced, flailing.

He struggled, trying to break free from the mess that ensnared his limb. Who knew layers of dirt didn't destroy the stickiness that originally came part and parcel with the web?

An arm should never look more like a Halloween prop than part of a body. He pulled his jacket off, using the remaining clean sections to remove any lingering remnants from the rest of him.

"Found it!" Ryder called out. The final chamber was the jail cell he had been sentenced to - nothing more than a place to rot while life passed him by. Not that it mattered. In the greater scheme of things, his life wasn't worth much anyways.

His jacket fell in one corner, slumping into a pile. The organizing had begun. He had a laundry pile. He took a second glance at it, wondering if he'd actually be allowed to do laundry.

He staggered, almost tripping over a single electrical cord. Its outlets were already full, one side powering the light and the other a small fridge. A single tug yanked the door open. At least his employers, whoever they were, had been good enough to give him a few things to eat and some bottled water.

Ryder collapsed on his new bed, wiggling from side to side. Somewhere there was a spot one spring or another didn't push through. He just had to find it - a task that was worse than being poked on social media. The cot squeaked its displeasure with every move. A psychic wasn't needed to predict a stiff neck was in his future. The paper-thin pillow was the first thing he planned to toss aside when his own belongings arrived... if they arrived.

He inhaled deeply, a stale boredom filling his senses - strong enough to make his eyelids grow heavy. His mouth distorted under the pressure of a yawn. A window would have been nice. He yawned again, rubbing his eyes at the same time.

Being stuck inside four walls was something he was used to, but being alone was devastating. At least outside this place, he had some company.

Amy. Was she alright?

Growing up alone was hard, especially with no friends. Amy had been in the same boat as him when they first met: abused, battered, bruised, and abandoned to her own means.

Children didn't deserve to be treated like that.

They latched onto each other immediately. He chuckled. Back then, they were two peas in a pod. It was only recently that their paths began to drift in opposite directions. Drugs had replaced him as her confident. That left a sour taste in his mouth and a feeling of inadequacy in his soul. Perhaps there was even a touch of jealousy hidden in there as well from the knowledge an addiction could claim his place so easily.

Their relationship was complicated at best, being more about his shortcomings than about either of their emotions. He liked Amy, but more importantly, he liked having her around. He even called her his girlfriend, but, in the end, the truth was he wasn't in love with her and he knew he never would be. That didn't make the few times they hooked up mistakes, though.

Amy had her own life that included other men and more often than not taking payment for certain services rendered. They had no secrets in that regard. He knew all about her side jobs and accepted them for exactly what they were - a means to an end. Money or even a job wasn't easy to come by for either of them, especially in their neighbourhood. He simply wasn't in any position to make things different for her.

How could he? He couldn't even hold a job with his record. Still, looking out for her as best he could was the least he could do. Their bond might not have been destined, but they needed each other just the same.

All people needed companionship. That was a fact of life. Those without, the ones the rest of society forgot about, were no different in that aspect. One didn't need to be in love to have the need to feel loved. That was what Amy and Ryder offered each other: a bit of comfort and someone to lean on when things turned sour.

Then things changed. Amy fell in with some shady individuals - the type that offered her a temporary escape from life's worst moments... for a price. It wasn't real. She even knew that. It didn't matter. The fact remained, drugs had a lot to offer the truly desolate. To some, anything was better than living another minute in reality.

Ryder tried everything he could think of to help her. It almost worked. Another few weeks and he might have managed to get her clean. That was when the incident happened.

In her state, Amy was fragile. She never would have survived a bout in jail. They both knew it. That was why Ryder accepted his fate and never tried to clear himself of the vandalism charges. The risk was too high that the police would have blamed Amy for what happened. If it was assumed he was guilty, there would be no need to go searching for the truth. Amy would be free and at least have a fighting chance. His being sent away for an entire year was going to be difficult for both of them. All he could do was hope she made good use of his sacrifice and stayed off the drugs while he was gone.

Ryder rubbed his eyes and face, worrying wasn't going to help. From where he lay, there was nothing he could do about the world passing him by. He had his own problems to deal with. How was he supposed to do a good job when he didn't know exactly what he was being asked to do? What would happen if he didn't do what was expected of him? A year was long enough. He couldn't imagine additional time being tacked onto his sentence.

He tossed a book in the air, catching it again as if it were a football. Reading was worse than having his fingernails pulled off one at a time and more likely to bring about tears.

He stood, deciding to pace. The book went up a little higher with each toss. With a bang, it crashed to the ground, pages folded and torn and spine misaligned.

Ryder blinked twice. "Oops," he said, covering his mouth and with it a chuckle trying to escape. "Guess that's why books aren't used in sports." He squatted beside the broken book, picking it up as carefully as possible - not that additional damage would have made much of a difference. It needed surgery at the hands of a book doctor extraordinaire. He glanced around. There wasn't one to be seen.

A piece of paper floated down, light as a feather lost from a bird flying overhead. Ryder alternated glances between the tiny sheet and what was left of the book - their colours completely different. That wasn't the only thing odd. The words that graced the front of the escapee parchment all appeared to be handwritten.

He traced the interior of the book. "Ow!" He shook his hand before putting his index finger in his mouth. Paper cuts were the worst. At least this one served a purpose, finding a rip in the inside jacket.

His lips curled up at the edges. Something so mysterious couldn't happen with a modern-day paperback. They lacked the technique and artistry that having been hand-bound added to truly creating a work of art from literature.

The tiny hole revealed a hidden compartment the creator had left to one day be discovered. Whatever the message logged on the paper was, it had been neatly tucked away - hidden since the book was first brought to life. Someone had thought it was important enough to stash for future generations.

He glanced at the book's inside information. There was no mention of a date of publication, or a publisher for that matter. It would have taken a forensic scientist to match a time period to the materials - all in the hopes of finding out how long someone's words had waited to be read out loud. The cot squeaked, the closed book landing in its center.

Ryder's fingers and thumb rubbed against each other, looking for resolve and finding just the right amount of courage. One hand reached out, grasping the scrap. It was crudely torn on one side and at least one piece was missing, probably more.

Air escaped his lips slowly. He stood, rubbing his neck where tiny hairs stood at attention. The temperature of the room dropped.

The key is only to be used

when true love fails

and one partner stands accused

Ryder spun around. He'd felt something coming towards him, but there was nothing there. He side-eyed the spot from which he felt the presence. The only thing out of the ordinary was the book now lying on the ground in a pile of shreddings made from its own pages.

A crash sounded from down the hall, drawing his attention. Without thought, Ryder rushed to the bottom of the stairs and a view of what was left of the door at the top, reduced to nothing more than a pile of toothpicks and scraps of firewood. Something had destroyed it, but what? And why?

Chapter Nine

A twinkle formed in Mirabelle's eyes, a reflection of the dangling prisms from the overhead chandelier. Ever since she first heard it was rumoured to be made entirely of precious gemstones, she dreamt about the day she would be able to see it in-person. If even a fraction of the stories she had heard were true, its value was far more than even she could imagine. That was a lot.

"It's beautiful," she mumbled, lost in grandiose splendor of the posh restaurant.

"It pales in comparison to you, my dear," Dante praised. "Come. I have a table reserved."

"How did you know we were coming?" Mirabelle questioned. "We only just met a few hours ago."

"I didn't," Dante admitted. "I always have a table ready should I need one. It's merely one of the perks of my position. It is owned by... those I work for."

Mirabelle's lips curled up. "For free?" she asked, side-eyeing her companion.

Dante laughed, holding out a chair for her. "Money has little value to me. It is irrelevant in the greater scope of things. We have our own system of rewards. This," he motioned around the room, "is one of them."

"That sounds wonderful," Mirabelle raved, allowing him to push her chair in under her.

"I am Maurice," a young waiter said, bowing, one hand in front of his midsection, the other behind. Between the man's thumb and first finger sat a lone match. The red tip struck against a black flint. The end flared, smoke rising. He leaned forward, allowing the flame to gently touch the edge of the candle wicks, bestowing each of them with a passionate and fiery kiss. Both sputtered in protest before agreeing to fulfill the purpose for which they were created. A golden hue radiated across the table, illuminating the faces of its guests.

"Thank you, Maurice," Dante said, nodding. "White wine for the lady and I'll have a cognac."

"Very good, sir," Maurice replied, walking backwards to exit.

Mirabelle's face lit up brighter than the candles. Drinking underage was against all the rules. Her parents hadn't even allowed her the occasional sip. With this man... her man, things were different. She was treated as an adult - an equal. This was the way she deserved to be treated, and she had no plans to go back to the rules and restrictions she had previously been forced to live with.

"I hope you don't mind me taking the liberty of ordering for you," Dante said.

"Not at all," Mirabelle gushed adoration in her reply.

"Now," Dante continued, "I believe you were going to tell me all about your problems."

Mirabelle giggled. "They seem so far away when I am with you." She paused, her hands wringing the napkin under the table. "My parents don't see me as you do."

The waiter returned with their drinks. "Are you ready to order?" He asked.

"No," Dante replied. "We'll need a few more minutes." He grasped the warmed snifter placed before him, swirling the caramel-coloured liquid inside. It was the perfect colour, no doubt darkened naturally from being properly aged in pure oak wood barrels.

With the edge of the glass almost touching his chin, he inhaled the dried fruit aromas that had concentrated at the top. The brim inched closer to his nostrils, each flaring its approval. The first sip was nothing more than a tease, enough to wet his lips, but allowing only the smallest amount to actually pass through. He closed his eyes, savouring the burn on the tip of his tongue. The corners of his mouth curled up - an offering of appreciation for the finely crafted french brandy.

He returned his attention to his guest. "You were saying?"

"My parents..."

"Ah, yes." Dante interrupted. "They don't respect you. It's a shame, really. Why go through the process of adoption if they didn't plan on treating you fairly?"

"Adoption?!" Mirabelle shrieked.

"Don't tell me they didn't even explain that to you!" Dante said, adding a *tsk tsk* on the end.

"No, they didn't," Mirabelle replied, the beginnings of a scowl taking form on her face. "Are you sure?"

"Quite," Dante answered. "It was big news years back. A couple of families perished in a rather large fire. I believe there were multiple houses lost and only two survivors, a boy and a girl. Your parents were somehow connected to it all... I'm not sure how. In the end, they decided to adopt, but took only one of the children. They chose you. I hope their recent attitudes aren't a result of some sort of regret about that decision."

"Who was the boy?" Mirabelle asked.

"I don't know him personally," Dante replied. "But I saw your father with him earlier... at the courthouse. I think I've seen them together a few times there." His glass pressed between his lips allowing the liquid to flow through, this sip considerably larger than the last.

"He blew me off to spend time with him," Mirabelle mumbled, her eyes pointed down, darting back and forth, searching for answers. "They do regret choosing me. That's why he is spending so much time with that boy. It isn't just work..."

"I'm sorry," Dante offered. "There is a way you could help me and get your revenge on them..."

"How?" Mirabelle asked, her frosty gaze cold enough to extinguish the candle flames.

"First, we eat," Dante announced, motioning for the waiter. "I have a surprise for you for dessert."

"What is it?" The disappointment in Mirabelle's eyes vanished. What girl didn't love a good surprise? "Tell me."

Dante laughed. "You are full of enthusiasm," he said, reaching into his suit jacket pocket. "This is for you - a small token of appreciation. Call it an advance... for agreeing to help me."

Mirabelle glanced at the box sitting pretty on the table, a red ribbon tied around its midsection, complete with dainty bow. "For me," she cooed, one hand pressed against her chest. Patience was a virtue someone forgot to give her. Her free hand reached out, snatching it up. The beautiful wrapping fell to the floor in pieces.

"I hope you like it," Dante said, taking his final sip of the cognac. "It's made from the same precious gems as the chandelier."

Mirabelle forced her jaw to close. "It's perfect," she said, flashing a toothy grin. "Will you put it on me?"

Dante rounded the table. He scooped her blonde hair to the side. Sliding the necklace around her neck, fastening the catch at the back. "You understand I need you to do something for me, don't you?"

"Anything." Mirabelle's hand caressed over her new acquisition. This was what she wanted. This was what she deserved. This man understood her perfectly.

"Good," Dante said, retaking his seat. "I need to run a few tests. They are very specific and only a certain genealogy will do." He held up one hand. "Before you offer, I am afraid it isn't as simple as volunteering yourself. I need three extremely specific people."

"How can I help with that?" Mirabelle questioned, holding out her necklace to admire it.

"I need you to deliver your parents and that boy to me," Dante explained. "After I have what I need, I'll make sure they know they never should have treated you the way they did."

Mirabelle's mouth curled up on one side, the twinkle in her eyes diamond shaped. "Do you promise?"

"Promise," Dante replied.

"Then I will help in any way I can," Mirabelle stated. "Can we eat now? I'm famished."

"Of course," Dante laughed. He motioned for the waiter to return.

Chapter Ten

Any clues that might have been left at the crime scene were long gone before Gabrielle arrived. Yellow police tape blew in the wind, having been stretched out earlier by any number of people holding it up in order to scoot underneath. A single policeman sat in his car, a doughnut in one hand and coffee in the other. The voice of a sportscaster calling plays for a local football game drowned out any other noises in the area.

Gabby watched from across the street. There was no sense mixing it up with local law enforcers when there wasn't a demon to be seen. Instincts told her to head towards the library. The one place that had always been the focal point of her trip was bound to hold at least a few answers. Everything else that had happened up until then had merely been a distraction aimed at throwing her off the trail. Hopefully, it hadn't gone completely cold.

She wrapped her arms around her midsection. With the sun's shift done for the day, the temperature was dropping quickly. It wasn't quite frigid enough to freeze her breath, but any exposed skin was taking a beating. Jack Frost was to blame, exhaling the cold gusts, all the while mocking those who were caught in his reach. Lowering her head, she pushed through. Not even nature could make her say uncle. Defeat had no place in any of the languages she spoke.

Trees whistled catcalls as she passed by. As if that wasn't enough, an owl hidden away in one of their knots joined in the chorus. She met the stare of its two yellow eyes dead-on, not veering until the nocturnal opponent blinked. It hooted a second challenge at her back. There was no need for a rematch, or even to glance behind acknowledging the request. She'd taken the first contest easily. Who knew birds of prey were sore losers?

The library stood out, a healthy thumb on a hand of broken fingers. The wind howled a warning in her ears. At its advice, she inhaled deeply, picking up the faint scent of demons. They were close.

Gabby stopped, the world appearing to join her. She glanced around, her top teeth marking an indent on her bottom lip. In the last few short paces she had taken, the air had grown thick. The rustling of the trees and even the owl were all memories left behind. The tiny hairs on her arms and the back of her neck stood at attention, eagerly awaiting the unveiling of unknown danger.

In one swift motion, she threw her body behind a bush, cautiously peeking back around. The doors to the library sat uneven, having been busted open. Two assailants fled down the sidewalk, too busy to notice they were being watched. That was sloppy, even for a demon.

Her eyes locked on, following their every move. Tracking was a gift she shared with her brothers. Hers, however, was the most advanced of the four. In her opinion, technology dulled their senses. She warned them from the beginning, but as always, none of them listened to her good advice. She might as well have been talking to a wall.

Her lack of use and her brothers' acceptance of it was the only explanation for the difference in their skill levels. Computer screens and ultra-violet lights affected the eyes in ways no one fully comprehended. Years from now, the damage might be more severe than even she had imagined.

Staying far back, she trailed the two runners to what, from the front yard, appeared to be an abandoned house. It was difficult to tell where plants ended and weeds began, all bunched together in clumps. Those that had flourished in warmer temperatures were now yellowed by death. Colourful petals had also succumbed to a bitter end, browned and crisp. Overgrown and unkempt, the longest creepers grabbed at her ankles as she passed by, protesting her invasion of the all but hidden path.

What was left of the front door hung off one hinge. She stepped through, trying not to disturb the wood. It was best not to outrage any history that might have been contently hidden within the walls. The house was deserted for a reason - one Gabrielle didn't need to know about.

Light on the feet brings a surprise to all you meet!

The oldest known residents of a once-happy family home were now rodents and spiders. She brushed aside cobwebs, exploring further inside. Missing pieces and holes in the staircase leading up, suggested that was not the route to follow. Still, the main level didn't seem plausible either. In layers of unscathed dust, there wasn't any sign of life, only shadowy silhouettes of what once might have been.

Gabby continued forward, taking note of every inch of ripped wallpaper that still remained, pasted over crumbling walls. A putrid odour of feces mixed with rot stung her nostrils - the smell strong enough to make her want to add her own vomit to the mix. She gagged, regretting her decision to throw down shots with Earl earlier in the day.

A door up ahead caught Gabrielle's attention. She inched closer, its bright blue handle taunting her - too shiny to be an original piece of decor. It had to have been placed there on purpose - a marker of sorts.

She composed herself, preparing for the worst. If the main level was a disaster, the basement was bound to be worse. Summoning courage, she flung open the door in one swift motion.

Light brightened the area around her. This wasn't what she had imagined would be found lurking below. The stairs, although wooden and poorly painted, were spotlessly clean. She tested her weight on the first step. It held. Using the banister for support, she took each step as a new challenge. She stifled a giggle when she reached the bottom. There had been no need for her extensive caution.

Gabrielle gasped. Someone had decked out the lower level in expensive fine furnishings. It was a complete opposite to what waited at the top of the stairs. On a table in the middle of the room sat a tray filled to the brim with different cheeses and matched with a bowl of assorted crackers. Half-full glasses of wine had been abandoned - their owners no doubt in an important meeting in one of the adjoining rooms.

She suppressed the urge to laugh, knowing exactly what she had walked in on. This was the meeting place of a lesser cult made up of a handful of harmless demons and a collection of mortals with a desire to become god-like. Typically, these fools didn't have the wherewithal to realize that was an impossibility. Gods were born, not mutated by some ritualistic magic. Their own ignorance made them easy targets for lies and promises that would never be fulfilled.

Why they wanted to be transformed into a demon in the first place was beyond her. Demons were hideous, especially their all-black bugged-out eyes. Not to mention, they also weren't on the higher end of the intellectual scale.

Gabby sighed. All it had taken was one person to sensationalize the entire demonic process and poof there was a lineup of power-hungry fools willing trade their souls for what they believed to be the upper hand.

Technology wasn't void of fault, either. It played its role, glorifying vampires and werewolves, along with countless other paranormal creatures. Movies had made it popular to be different and being a monster was definitely different.

Dante! It had to be him. The more she thought about it, the more money she was willing to bet. He was as sly as they came and had an intellect to boot. Michael had mentioned Dante's fingers were dangling in several cookie jars. What better way to make a statement and money at the same time than through media, movies, books and music?

She shook her head, needing her full focus on the here and now. Instincts led her to a closed set of doors, the same blue colour handle she'd seen before mocking her in an open invitation. This was one party she wasn't about to refuse.

The doors swung open. The scent of burning incense was the first to attack, her nostrils the victims. They were losing this battle. Her nose threatened a sneeze, upset by the undeserved bombardment it was being subjected to. One thing was for sure, it was going to be a long time before she'd be stopping to smell the roses again.

The newest chamber was laid out in the same manner as every demon-worshiping cult that came before it. Apparently, sect décor was the one thing that hadn't changed throughout the ages.

She was seeing red, literally. The carpet, the walls, their cloaks and even the altar linen all boasted the same colour reminiscent of fresh blood. Taking stock of the situation, she aged the group as being brand new on the scene. It wasn't what was there, but rather what wasn't there that divulged the clan's secret. There weren't any fading or scuff marks from extended use on the carpets. If anything, she might have stumbled upon one of their first meetings. Of course, she was also going to make it their last.

"Sorry to disturb!" Gabby lied. "I need to ask you a few questions." One hand reached to her side, unsheathing her sword. Its white and gold surface reflected back at her from the centre of black eyes. "We can do this the easy way..."

There was nothing worse than a demon shriek; not even nails on a chalkboard could compare to their horrific garble of high-pitched sounds. Gabby's teeth clenched together, grinding. Her sword raised vertically before her, she caressed the flat side with one open palm.

"I guess not," Gabby said. "Gladia, my friend, I need you." The molecules of the blade began to morph, changing to grains of golden sand before twisting and turning into a new form.

"Ah!" a demon screamed, sprinting towards her. "You have no place here, demigod! Begone!"

Gabrielle's lips turned upwards. She released her grasp on her weapon, the hilt lunging forward in the shape of a snake. Fangs pierced the demon's skin, sending it shrieking to the ground, body convulsing in a seizure. Gladia took aim at a second foe, doing the same damage to it. The hissing python cleared the room of all but two cloaked figures before slithering back to its owner. Gabby lowered her hand. Her companion coiled around, head facing their enemies, its forked tongue spitting hatred in every direction.

"I wouldn't try it if I were you," Gabby suggested, watching one of the two robed figures glance towards the exit. "They never listen." She sighed. "Gladia!"

No sooner than the attempted escape began, it was over. The snake sprung forward, picking up momentum as it flew through the air, transforming into a spear mid-flight before piercing the runaway's heart straight through.

"I told you not to try it," Gabby stated, shaking her head. "You won't be so silly, now will you?"

The hood of the cloak on the remaining cult member shook, falling backwards. Two women stood eye-to-eye amidst a room full of dead bodies. "What do you want from me?" she asked, her voice shaking.

"Some answers," Gabby replied, retrieving the spear. She wiped the still-warm blood off onto the deceased man's robes to which it belonged. "Why did demons kill that lawyer earlier?"

"We had nothing to do with that," the woman answered. "Orders came from high up. Someone else responded."

"Okay then," Gabby continued. "Why did your little clan break into the library?" She held up one hand. "Before you try to deny involvement, That's how I found your little hideout. I followed the perpetrators here. I already know you were behind it."

The woman bit her bottom lip. "They'll kill me," she pleaded. "If I betray them, I'm dead."

"If you don't answer me," Gabby replied, "you're dead. Either way, I guess you aren't making it through the night." She lifted her spear to the woman's neck. "I could call back my slithering friend to do it. I hear being digested by a python is an excruciating way to go. Gladia!"

The long white and gold snake slithered around Gabby's arm, its eyes focused on the woman in front of it. It hissed, inching closer, whispering messages of the brutality it had planned.

"Alright!" the woman screamed. "There is something of value in the library. The top of all the orders is rumoured to be offering important positions to any group who manages to retrieve it. Being located as close as we are, we thought we could beat the others to the punch."

"What is it exactly that you were tasked with retrieving?" Gabrielle questioned.

The woman opened her mouth, but before any words formed, a stream of blood flowed out. Air whizzed by Gabrielle's ear, a bullet kissing her hair as it passed by, lodging in the woman's forehead. A second one hit her midsection. Her body fell in a lump on the ground, joining the rest of her clan in death's icy grip.

Gabby spun around, but saw no one. There was only one thing to do: head back to the library and find whatever it was the demons wanted - before they did.

Chapter Eleven

Ryder stood fast at the bottom of the stairs, staring up at the broken door. There was a decision to be made and quickly. As always, it came down to which ear's advice to listen to, the ones whispered by curiosity or from common sense. Those two troublemakers were constants, one perched on each shoulder - the perfect vantage point to whisper their advice while bickering over most of the situations that popped up in his life. Given their track record, neither could be trusted, especially when in agreement.

He weighed his options, choosing to brush them both off as he would pesky flakes of dandruff. Their silence wouldn't last long. Both would return with a vengeance - a headache the price to pay for his insolence.

The urge to climb the stairs and investigate was gone, at least for the time being. At best, all that awaited above were the group of thugs that had broken in and another beating. He felt his nose, still swollen and tender. The old broad exiting the building had already done a bang-up job on him. He didn't need to add to the bruises.

If, for some reason, that scenario didn't happen, and he managed to escape the grasp of those actually responsible for the break-in, there was sure to be a video camera to catch his image clearly. That was all the proof any judge this side of the world needed to convict him of yet another crime he had nothing to do with.

The trudge back down the corridor seemed longer than the previous one, every tiny sound amplified a hundred-fold. Here, alone in the dark, his unblemished public facade was stripped away. There was no one to impress but himself and he was the only one who knew exactly what he was - a fraud.

He lived in a part of the world most of society turned its back on, refusing to acknowledge its existence. They were the poor; the underprivileged; the desolate; the desperate; the ones who had nothing left to lose. There was no aid coming to those living in squalor right in the backyard of politicians and debutantes. No one wanted to admit that the great nation they lived in had a problem. Even less wanted the burden of fixing conditions that rivaled the problems found in some third world countries. It was easier to turn a blind eye and pretend it wasn't real. It wasn't fair, but then he had learnt a long time ago life never was.

He pushed the one wooden chair in his quarters against the door, a trick he learnt moving from place to place and never knowing who had an extra set of keys. The barricade wouldn't last long, but at least there would be some notice if the goons returned looking for more loot.

Waiting for impending doom was always the worst, whether in a courtroom or knowing a beatdown was coming. Butterflies collided in his stomach. Of all the feelings a person could have, fear was the only one that couldn't be conquered. It came, invited or not, and planted itself in its host's favourite chair until it was good and ready to leave on its own accord. Any offering of food, polite or not, simply prolonged its stay. No one in their right mind wanted that.

He inhaled, his breath shaky and lips quivering. One of these days he wasn't getting up from being on the losing end of a beatdown. There would come a time when he would give up hope, but it hadn't happened yet. Despite all his adversities, he still wanted to live. There was still a glimmer of hope that one day he'd find something or someone worth living for.

The first clash Ryder dismissed. As much as he tried to convince himself the second clamour was no different, logic wasn't buying it. It had been louder; closer. By the third commotion, it was undeniable.

Each room was systematically being searched, or rather ransacked, by someone or something that wasn't happy about not finding whatever it was they wanted. All that grief and frustration would be taken out on his hide if they found him. He held his breath, hoping silence would be a good deterrent to the invaders. Perhaps they would give up and stop wasting their time in the dingy basement before coming to the last room. That was wishful thinking and his wishes never came true.

He let his jaw open, not allowing his teeth to touch, for fear their chattering might expose his location. It was too late. The door shook, struggling against the chair. This was it.

Bottles of water became his only ammo. He grabbed one in each hand and stood back, an arm poised in the air, waiting for the opportune moment. Theoretically, a shot to the head in the right place could knock a person out. He'd learnt that from his first stay in the joint. Prisoners knew how to make a weapon out of just about anything if they had to. Survival was the only rule worth following when incarcerated.

The chair crumbled to splinters under the pressure of the latest assault. The door flung wide open. Every muscle froze, taken captive by those hypnotic soulless black pools he knew so well.

Those eyes sucked his breath and strength away. There was nothing human about them; no conscience lay hidden beneath their gazes. Until that very moment, he hadn't known what real fear was. There was a big difference between feeling their power from behind and a face-to-face staredown in the most up-close and personal manner imaginable.

Water splashed on his shoes and pants. The single defence he had been relying on now lay in puddles, the liquid streaming away to find cracks to hide in.

He blinked, expecting to see his life flash before his eyes, but there was no slide show. It all came down to this. His pathetic life would come to an end in a dismal dungeon. No one would know he was gone or care. He'd simply cease to exist.

There were at least three of them, but his gaze locked on the figure closest.

Those eyes!

He'd never been hypnotized before and if this was what it felt like, he never wanted to experience it again. Knots formed in his stomach, tightening with every passing moment. He gasped, the air itself lacking the oxygen he so desperately needed. A feeling of helplessness washed over his body. Water formed in the corners of his eyes, not from tears, but the stinging pain of the strain that accompanied lids being held open against their will.

The front man took a step closer, what little light there was perfectly highlighted the rest of his gruesome features - using shadows to play havoc with Ryder's mind. If this was a costume only the best makeup artist could have produced something so intense - disgusting yet deadly beautiful at the same time. The nameless creature might as well have walked off the set of the latest horror movie... the type that left some folks screaming in fear and others begging for a chance to become one.

Vampire!

Ryder had never been one to put faith in the paranormal. His belief went as far as the drive-in movies on a Saturday night in the summer - if the opportunity arose to sneak in. The only way to know for sure if it was truly an undead creature of the night was if it opened its mouth. Those trademark fangs were a dead giveaway.

Another bang sounded from the hallway and he got what he asked for. The figure distorted its face as if in pain before its lips parted, allowing a high-pitched shriek to escape.

Ryder fell to his knees, hands covering his ears. His attacker definitely had fangs, except a full mouth of them - each one looking as if it had been sharpened by hand. A vampire it wasn't.

Demon!

Ears still ringing, he fell backwards, landing smack dab in the middle of the remnants of the water that had failed to protect him. It could have been vials of the holy variety, he doubted it would have made a difference. His faith was shaky at best to start with. As far as he was concerned, in today's society, the sight of one of these things would have sent even the holiest of priests packing for the hills.

He watched the three turn their attention to the door, each slowly backing towards him. There was another threat in the basement, but it wasn't him. Truth be told, it never was.

A reputation was what kept him safe most of the time without ever having to land a punch. He was fingered as the culprit of many an assault and took the fall, mainly out of fear of retribution. Those acts sat well with his peers. Before he knew it, he had been built up as a badass that no one wanted to mess with. Those who did came at him in groups and with weapons. Taking a beating and walking away only added to his notoriety. He'd been lucky in that regard.

The ruckus continued outside the doorway. Shadows flew by, their form unknown. Ryder scooted back to the wall, expecting a massive brute to explode through any time claiming to be a hunter of the dead. Instead, he found himself doing a double take.

A woman!

He was being rescued by a girl. Not just any female, either. She was radiant... and strong. One of his assailants landed in a heap on the floor beside him, groaning.

"Ow!" Ryder exclaimed, pinching himself. This wasn't a dream, but it felt like one.

Her hair, tied back in a ponytail, flipped around in slow motion. It was her own personal whip, adding a little extra humiliation to every opponent she bested. In a word, she was a goddess and he would have no problem worshiping her - preferably not from afar.

Ryder wasn't sure how many assailants the woman had singlehandedly taken on, but it was clear only those in the room with him remained. The one beside him staggered to his feet, joining the other two in a final stand of sorts.

"You boys are out of practice," she purred, her lips turning up ever so slightly, mocking her foes.

The pearlesque luster of her sword reflected what little light there was. Holding it vertically, almost touching her nose, her free hand caressed one side of the blade.

"A knife?" Ryder blurted out, quickly covering his mouth afterwards. That earned him a side glance and a chuckle.

"Would you prefer something with more of a bang?" she asked. "My friend, it's time to play. Show us what you can do."

Ryder's head shook. He blinked several times. He'd seen more in one night than the rest of his life combined. Who knew all these things actually existed? Creatures, fangs, some sort of a medieval fight and now magic all rolled up together in one big package and tied with a pretty bow. The best fantasy writer couldn't have thought this up.

The sword disappeared, replaced by a hand gun made from the same pearlesque shimmer.

"It doesn't matter what the weapon," she stated.

The gun transformed into an arrow, whizzing through the air. All three figures fell to the ground. Ryder's eyes crossed, staring at the sharp point as the arrow stopped mid-air, almost touching his nose.

"What are you looking for?" she asked. "Who do you work for? Speak or I shall have your tongue as a trophy."

"What?" Ryder replied. "I'm not looking for anything. I'm supposed to be sorting through the books down here. Keeping a tongue as a trophy is rather sick, don't you think?"

She glanced down at his wet crotch. "Damn. I would have kept one of them alive if I had known you were just a sniveling human."

Ryder glanced down. "No!" he exclaimed. "This isn't pee. It's water. I was planning on throwing the bottles. Why am I explaining this to you? I don't even know who you are."

"I'm the chick who just saved your ass," she smirked, lowering her arm to the base of the arrow, allowing it to disappear.

"Great," Ryder complained, He jumped to his feet, brushing off his clothing as best he could. He threw his arms in the air. "Anyone else going to come through the door and bust the place up tonight?"

"Gabrielle," she said, examining the room. "Did they say anything to you? Maybe what they were looking for? Why they broke into the library?"

"Nope," Ryder replied. "I don't think they were in the talking mood. It was more all grunts and then shrieks."

"Have you seen anything unusual?" Gabby asked.

"What do you mean by unusual?" Ryder replied, motioning around the room. "None of this is normal in my world. People don't have fangs or carry weapons that can transform into different things when you yell at them."

Gabby sighed. "A hidden compartment, or something carved into the stone?"

"Maybe," Ryder answered. "What's it worth to you? I might have something in my possession."

Gabby laughed. "Typical man, always the greedy ones. I could kill you and search your body myself," she threatened, pausing. "Alright, if it's a reward you are looking for, it's a reward you shall have. I'll take you with me and if you actually do have something to show me, you will be compensated appropriately. If you don't, I'll kill you... fair?"

"Not really," Ryder replied. "But seems I don't have much to negotiate with."

"No," Gabby agreed. "You really don't."

Chapter Twelve

"Tell me again why we are walking," Ryder complained. "Shouldn't you have a motorcycle or some cool car? I thought you were a superhero or something."

"I don't drive," Gabby replied, stopping to face her shadow. "Since we are technically escaping, perhaps you should try being a little more quiet. Or perhaps you would rather face another group like we did back at the library... or worse."

Ryder pursed his lips together tightly. His thumb and first finger made a locking motion in one corner, before throwing away the imaginary key. He waggled his eyebrows.

Gabby shrugged off his antics, turning to continue their trek and forcing a scowl onto her face. Finding him amusing and letting him know that she did were two different things. A good warrior knows not to let anyone privy to potential weaknesses. She glanced over her shoulder, acknowledging that a susceptibility was exactly what this stranger was becoming; a vulnerable spot in her impeccably designed armour - her own personal Achilles' heel.

"Where are we going?" Ryder asked.

"I thought you zipped and locked it," Gabby replied, keeping her pace.

"I don't think it's too much to ask where you are taking me," Ryder complained. "I'm going with you willingly and let's face it... I don't know the first thing about you. You could be a mass murderer. Actually, you are a mass murderer, if you consider the rather large pile of bodies we just left behind. Wouldn't you agree?"

Gabby stopped, this time keeping her back facing him. "You know what I think?"

"I wouldn't ask if I did," Ryder replied, snorting.

"I think you like the sound of your own voice a little too much," Gabby said, pursing her lips together to stop them from curling up. "If I wanted you dead, you'd already be dead."

Ryder held up his hands. "No arguments there," he said. "You could kick my ass."

"How about you keep that in mind next time you want to chat," Gabby suggested.

"For sure," Ryder agreed. "Just so you know, I'm pretty good at taking an ass whooping. I'm not just tooting my own horn. I seriously could have made a career out of being beaten to a pulp."

Gabrielle coughed, trying to cover up uncontrolled laughter. "Can we get going before we are attacked again?"

"Yeah," Ryder answered, pausing for a few minutes. "I made you laugh."

"Really," Gabby complained. "You are going to gloat over me finding you ridiculous?"

Ryder sighed. "A guy's gotta take what he can."

"Sh," Gabby said.

"Back to the sh-ing... great." He rolled his eyes.

Gabby shook her head, putting one finger to her lips. With Ryder tucked safely behind and body poised, she began the hunt, searching out possible predators lying in wait. Every muscle flexed, ready to pounce like a super feline ninja. This kitty, however, wasn't interested in playing nice. She had one thing in mind: the total annihilation of her target. She was in no mood to toy with her prey.

The hairs on the back of her neck stood up. This wasn't going to be an easy fight. She glanced from side to side, sizing up which group would make it to them first.

"Damn!" Gabrielle mumbled. "There are too many of them. They are coming at us from every direction."

"Funny," Ryder said, clinging to her back, "I had you pegged for as a one-against-all type of gal."

"There isn't anything funny about this," Gabby replied. "I am good, but even I can't beat some numbers games. There are two groups approaching from the left, one in front, one to the right and at least two more in your direction. I anticipate there are a dozen or more enemies in each group."

"You have some sort of plan though, right?" Ryder asked. "A gal like you always has a plan and a back-up too."

"Nope," Gabrielle replied. "I'm pretty much winging it. If you have anything that could help, now might be the time." She shuffled sideways. "Gladia!"

Ryder glanced over his shoulder. "A snake!" he exclaimed. "That thing is a snake too?!"

"Don't tell me you are afraid of snakes, too?" Gabby said, rolling her eyes. "Gladia, to the left!"

The snake flew through the air, transforming mid-flight into an arrow. Four attackers fell to the ground, lifeless. Gabby held out her hand, her weapon returning to a coiled position around her arm.

"Has any one ever told you how frightening you are?" Ryder asked. "It's remarkable... really!"

"This isn't the time for flattery," Gabrielle chuckled, adrenaline rushing through her veins at an all-time high. "Be more afraid of what's to come. Gladia can only do so much." Another transformation left a sword in her hand. "Stay back!"

Rushing forward, she met the first group head-on. Metal clashed on metal as she swirled around, wielding her blade against multiple opponents. A second group approached. They would be upon her in seconds.

*****

Ryder glanced around. He needed something he could use as a weapon. It didn't matter what, although he hoped it would be better than water bottles.

He clawed at a medium-sized boulder, partially hidden under bushes in a park garden behind him. Dirt filled his nails as he dug away at the ground surrounding its base, yet it refused to budge.

Gabrielle wasn't going to be able to hold them off of him for much longer. He scooted backwards under the bush, but it was too late to avoid being noticed. A stray attacker headed his way, fangs barred and saliva dripping from his mouth.

Ryder grimaced. Their chances of survival looked bleak. He glanced at Gabrielle, giving everything to protect him.

Coward!

She was amazing in every way: confident; strong; resourceful; beautiful. He felt a warmth radiating from his chest. Ryder sighed. "Love." He placed one hand over the spot, savouring the feeling, possibly the last emotion he would ever know.

His eyes shifted from side to side. A warmth crept over his hand, except the heat wasn't coming from his heart. One hand eagerly dove into his pocket, retrieving the torn piece of paper he had found earlier.

"The key is only to be use when true love fails and one partner stands accused!" he bellowed.

Ryder fell backwards, his hands covering his ears to no avail. Through watering eyes, he glanced up. Gabrielle appeared unaffected by the deafening sounds that plagued him - an untamed power that seized control of both his body and mind. Even in their retreat, the shrieks and howls echoed in vibrations across the park, stronger than the bellowing thunder of a god's anger.

Gabrielle pulled him to his feet by one arm. She glanced at each side of his head, nodding afterwards. A single finger pressed to his lips, silencing words yet to be formed.

Ryder rubbed his eyes. A hundred or more tiny drummers played to the rhythm of their own beat, using his mind as their instrument. Hopefully, wherever he was being led had painkillers and lots of them.

Losing any of one's senses wasn't easy. He'd taken them for granted: being able to hear; see; talk; smell; and touch. No one ever thought about a day coming when one of the five simply disappeared. This was a mere taste of what some people lived a lifetime experiencing. After this, he would have a new respect for those who survived daily and overcame disabilities.

He wasn't completely void of sounds. Someone simply turned the volume down to its lowest setting. Human nature was an odd thing. Knowing he couldn't make out every spoken word made him strain harder to hear the smallest details, all the while knowing his actions were causing his head additional pain.

It was a normal reaction to an abnormal situation. When one smelled something bad, one tended to take a second, deeper whiff. When one couldn't make out the details of an object far away, one tried harder, obsessed to know that which was hidden from their sight. Curiosity was as deadly as any sin.

Gabby's grip tightened around his arm, either trying to force him to quicken his pace or attempting to take his blood pressure. He wasn't sure which. With little effort, she propelled him forwards, concrete steps becoming a landing strip. He was a wheel-less plane trying to crash in the best possible manner. By the time he glanced up, she was already leaps and bounds ahead.

Scrambling to his feet, Ryder followed, only coming to the realization of where they were as he took the final step. "The courthouse?!" he yelled, still not able to gauge tempo properly. "It's closed!"

Gabrielle simply rolled her eyes. The front door opened as easily as if it were the middle of the day.

Ryder alternated glances between her and the open door that led to another bout of the unknown. Deep inside, he knew his life would never be the same if he stepped beyond that threshold. Did he enter? Could he trust Gabrielle? A beautiful woman had caused the downfall of many a man, especially when it came to his sanity.

A light pat on the back turned into a hard push. The choice having been made for him, Ryder stumbled through to the other side. Landing on his hands and knees once again, he glanced up directly into the face of a stranger.

"I see we have company," Michael said.

Gabrielle stepped over him. "Yeah. He has something that could be important. You mind dragging him to the other room? I've had enough hauling dead weight for one day."

Chapter Thirteen

"Can't we go any faster?" Mirabelle complained.

"Relax," the driver of the car said. "She's out cold." He glanced in his rear view mirror. "What did you do to her, anyways?"

"I ground up some of her sleeping pills and added the powder to her tea," Mirabelle confessed. "I had to pull off an award-winning performance, begging for forgiveness for my ill manners as of late." Her tongue pressed against the inside of her cheek, forming a bulge on her face.

"Looks like it worked," he commented. "I'm Luke, by the way. I guess you figured out I am one of Dante's drivers."

"Mirabelle," she blurted out. Idle chat with one of Dante's boy-Fridays wasn't how she planned her day to progress, but it would have to do. She'd bide her time until she was reunited with her true love.

She gave the driver a once-over. He was obviously a tad bit older than her, since he was driving. The acne around his nose and chin, however, suggested he was probably still in his teens. Other than that, there wasn't anything noticeable about him. Every detail about the boy's appearance was average, from his medium-length light brown hair to his height and weight. Even his eyes were a common shade of brown. He could have been the guy next door or the one down the street.

"He's amazing," Luke continued, interrupting her thoughts. "Dante, I mean. Imagine being alive for centuries."

"What?!" Mirabelle exclaimed.

"Freaky, right," Luke continued. "I wouldn't have believed it either except this was my dad's job and before him, my grandfather's. I can tell you he hasn't aged a day in all that time. Rumour has it he was around at the creation of the world. It's a hush-hush topic, though. You might not want to go poking around about it or anything."

"How is that possible?" Mirabelle asked, lines of worry aging her as the seconds passed by. If she grew old and Dante didn't...

"Apparently, he drinks blood," Luke stated. "I get wanting to be immortal and all, but I'm not sure I could drink it, especially fresh." He stuck his tongue, motioning with one finger inside his open mouth.

"Like a vampire?" Mirabelle chuckled.

"Not exactly," Luke replied. "He doesn't have fangs or anything, and from what I understand, the blood can only come from certain family lines."

"You mean it's a genetic thing?" Mirabelle mumbled. "He probably has to run a bunch of tests and stuff."

"Yeah, something like that," Luke answered. "We're almost to the old mine. I don't mean to pry, but weren't there supposed to be two others? Dante hates jobs being part done, if you know what I mean."

"Huh," Mirabelle muttered. "Right. I have that covered." She brushed her bangs off her face, tucking the strands behind one ear. The buttons on her phone beeped as she tapped her instructions.

"Hello," Merv said, answering.

"Daddy!" Mirabelle cried. "Daddy, you have to help us!"

"Mirabelle!" Merv exclaimed. "What's wrong? Where are you? I'll come get you right away!"

"They said they'll kill us if you don't do what they want!" Mirabelle blurted out. "You have to help us!"

"Okay, baby," Merv answered. "Tell me what to do. I promise, I'll do whatever it takes to keep you safe."

"They want you to bring the boy... the one from the courthouse. You need to bring him to the old mine just outside town. They say you have to come alone!" Mirabelle shrieked. "Daddy, don't let them hurt us!"

"I won't," Merv stated. "Is your mother with you?"

"Yes," Mirabelle whined. "But she's passed out. I think they drugged her. Daddy, I'm scared." She clicked end.

Luke glanced at her from the side. "You're good," he praised. "It doesn't bother you turning over your own parents?"

"They aren't really my parents," Mirabelle blurted out. "They never were."

Chapter Fourteen

"So what is this place?" Ryder asked, rubbing his jaw. A mouth full of tile wasn't a good diet, even if it did look like it was imported from the fanciest of regions. Everything there did and that wasn't necessarily a good thing. A klutz seldom fared well around expensive art pieces, especially breakable ones. He held his breath, following in his hosts' footsteps.

"Have a seat," Michael ordered, pulling out a chair. "This is the library."

"Funny," Ryder chuckled. "I figured that out from all the bookshelves filled with... books."

Michael flashed a glare before turning to his sister. "Who is this guy? It's not like you to bring home strays."

"This is Ryder," Gabby replied. "He has something I need to examine." She held out her hand.

Ryder dug deep into his pocket, producing the torn scrap that had already saved his life at least twice. "I can have it back, right?" He lifted his arm, holding the paper in the air behind him.

"Thank you," Tara said, snatching it from his grip from behind.

"Hey!" Ryder complained. "That's not fair."

Michael rolled his eyes. "If we are done playing games," he said, pausing. "Perhaps we can move things along."

Tara placed the tattered piece into Gabby's open hand. "This what you needed?" she asked, ignoring Michael.

"Can someone please fill me in on what is going on?" Ryder complained.

"I'm Tara and this is Michael... Gabby's brother." She rounded the table and took a seat beside Michael, knocking his feet off the table, to which he growled a response.

"I have been attacked by vampires..."

"Demons," Gabrielle corrected without looking up from her examination.

"Fine!" Ryder exclaimed. "I was attacked by demons, saved by a woman whose sword can change into a gun or a snake... I personally hate snakes, by the way, although probably not as much as demons. I barely escaped with my life at least twice..."

"You were fine," Gabby interrupted.

"Not fine!" Ryder argued. "There were too many of them. Then I read that paper; they all screamed; I lost my hearing and got dragged through the courthouse door, except it led to this place instead."

"You seem to be hearing fine now," Gabrielle stated.

"Yeah," Ryder agreed. "Why is that? I need some answers."

"You won't believe us," Gabrielle replied.

"Try me," Ryder demanded. "With all I have been through today, I doubt there is anything left that could surprise me."

"Okay," Michael said, clasping his hands together on the table between them. "Gabrielle, our two brothers, and myself were tasked with a job by the creator of this world. We have existed almost as long as existence itself. You may have heard of us... the Four Horsemen."

"The Four Horsemen," Ryder said, pursing his lips together and sticking them out. "As in... of the Apocalypse?"

"Those would be them," Michael said, grinning.

Ryder raised one finger in the air. "So what you are telling me," he started, "is that, in this world that I somehow managed to stumble into, there aren't any good guys." He held his finger up again. "Wait... wait. I want to see if I have this straight. Demons are obviously bad." He paused long enough to receive a nod. "And they are fighting with you... the Four Horsemen, to see who can unleash Hell on Earth first."

Michael shook his head. "Don't believe everything you read. We aren't the bad guys. From the beginning, our job has been to keep the gates to Hell closed and locked. Throughout the ages we somehow ended up with a bit of a bad rap."

"I can't imagine how that could happen," Ryder said, rolling his eyes. "Oh wait! Yes I can. Maybe it's all the killing..."

"Do we need him alive?" Michael asked, glancing over at his sister. "I could take care of him quickly. Say the word!"

"Unfortunately," Gabby replied, "we do need him alive."

"See," Ryder said, snapping his fingers. "That's exactly what I was talking about."

"Are you sure, Gabrielle?" Michael questioned, raising his brow. "Positive?"

"Yes! I am positive we need him." Gabby replied. "I thought this was part of one of the scrolls, but now I think it is something else. He somehow managed to use the words written on it to scare off demons. What I don't understand is how he read it. It's handwritten in a language that predates even us. This could be the original language of the gods, from before this world ever existed."

Ryder crossed his hands in front of his chest, giving Michael a single nod and a wink. "Yeah, that's right. You need me," he mocked. "Wait! What?" He reached over and grabbed the paper. "It looks normal to me. It certainly isn't a foreign, god-like language."

It was Michael's turn to snatch the scrap. "It's gibberish. I can't read it," he said, passing it to Tara.

"Nope," Tara agreed. "I have no clue what that says. It looks like a bunch of little pictures lined up."

Ryder glanced from face to face, wagging his finger at each of them. "Very funny. Okay guys, great joke."

"Nobody else is laughing," Michael stated. "I think Gabrielle is correct. This could be the language of the gods."

"Why would I see an unknown vocabulary? And why would it appear in words I recognize? I'm not a scholar. I didn't even finish high school, for crying out loud." Ryder searched the eyes of each companion.

"That's the question, isn't it?" Gabrielle replied. "Until we have an answer, you are going to be our house guest. We'll get you settled in a spare room and find you a change of clothes."

"Wallet," Michael said, holding out his hand.

"What?" Ryder complained. "You live in a place like this and want to rob me?"

"Don't be an idiot," Michael snarled.

Ryder huffed. Standing, he retrieved the folded holder from his back pocket. The map of lines worn into the once dark-brown leather, showed his journey through life. Inside, tucked safely away, was his whole existence. Dismissing all of that to hand it over to a total stranger felt wrong, or more to the point, didn't feel right. It was his friend; his companion.

"Any time would be good," Michael complained.

Ryder forced a smile, tossing it onto the table, rather than placing it in the palm of a stranger.

"Thank you," Michael scoffed, unfolding it. After removing the items he was looking for, he tossed it back on the table.

"Why do you need my identification?" Ryder questioned.

"To see who you are and how you fit in to all of this," Michael replied. "Where is your family?"

Ryder pursed his lips together, an emptiness filling his eyes. "Dead," he said, shrugging his shoulders.

"Siblings?" Michael asked.

"None."

"Aunts? Uncles? Relatives of any kind?" Michael pressed on.

"Nope," Ryder said. "It's just me."

"Okay. I'll be back." Michael slid out of his seat, planting a kiss on Tara's forehead before leaving the room.

Chapter Fifteen

"I still don't understand what any of this has to do with me," Ryder said, pacing in circles around the long table. Every so often, he glanced down at his own reflection in the perfect polish of the wooden surface.

"That's what Michael has gone to find out," Tara replied. "I know this is hard, but everything will work out."

"Right," Ryder snorted.

"Believe it or not, I was where you are sitting now not long ago," Tara explained. "Michael saved my life, just like Gabby saved yours. I was as confused as you must be right now."

"Almost the same," Gabby interrupted.

"Right," Tara said, giggling. "My situation is a bit different. I hit demons with flowers to make them run away."

"Excuse me," Ryder said, raising one eyebrow. "Flowers? Who thinks this stuff up?"

"A god did," Gabby growled. "Moreover the god who created the world you live in did."

"So that means I shouldn't question the sanity behind it?" Ryder asked. "As a god he could have given her a better weapon that a bouquet or some long-lost poetry."

Tara laughed. "I agree. It all seems rather silly. We are born of the bloodline and given an odd skill set to protect us from demons."

"Bloodline?" Ryder echoed.

"Don't get too friendly," Michael ordered, returning with a thick file in his hand. "This fella has a rap sheet a mile long."

"Right," Ryder replied, nodding. "And if you believe everything you read, I know some history books on your own achievements that might be insightful."

"Touché," Michael answered. "Still, I'd like to know how all this happened."

"My parents died in a fire," Ryder explained. "I bounced around from foster home to foster home. If something went wrong, I was blamed and shipped off to another place. If enough people tell you an apple is bad, odds are you won't bother to taste it to find out for yourself. You simply throw it away without thinking twice. Why go through the effort? That's my life in a nutshell. Anytime I get accused, I am automatically found guilty."

Michael sat flipping through the pages of the file. "So why aren't you in jail?"

"I have a good lawyer," Ryder explained, examining a few books on a side table. "Merv was friends with my parents. He always said he felt an obligation to look out for me. I've had minimal experiences in lock-up because of him."

Gabrielle's gaze followed him. "Were you in court yesterday?" she asked.

"Yeah," Ryder admitted. "I took the fall on a vandalism charge for someone. That's why I was at the library, serving community service. It's better than what the other side wanted - a full psych evaluation at some institution. Can you say lobotomy?"

"He didn't get what they wanted," Gabby mumbled in barely more than a whisper. "That's why they killed him."

"What?!" Ryder shrieked.

"Yeah," Gabrielle said. "The prosecutor is dead. That happened before the library was broken into."

"Do you think Dante has something to do with all this?" Michael asked.

"Who is Dante?" Ryder asked.

"He used to be a friend of theirs, but then there was a falling out, so to speak," Tara explained.

Michael grimaced at her choice of words. "She has the falling part right. He fell off a mountain."

"We searched for him... his body," Gabrielle continued, "but never found it. We presumed him dead. Until..."

"He tried to kill me," Tara finished.

"What's this guy look like?" Ryder asked.

"There is a likeness of him right beside you," Michael stated. "That was before photographs were invented."

Ryder glanced at the portrait. "This guy," he whined. "You're telling me that Amy's lawyer is behind the attack on my life?"

"You've seen him recently?" Michael questioned, raising his brow.

"Yeah," Ryder replied. "He comes around to see Amy all the time... well, at least twice a week."

"Who is Amy?" Gabby asked.

"My girlfriend," Ryder replied. "She lives next door to me in the housing complex. Well, did until I was sentenced to the library basement for a year."

Gabby forced a smile. A lump in her throat prevented her from uttering even a single word. At the same time, her stomach churned, threatening to erupt at any time. A cold sweat formed on the back of her neck, simultaneously with a stinging pain in her eyes.

She hadn't even thought to ask if he had a girlfriend before letting her shield down enough to get hurt. That was a mistake she wouldn't make again. Swallowing all of her emotions, she pulled herself together.

"I can go check things out," Michael offered.

"No," Gabby argued. "I'll do it. You need to stay here and watch over Tara... and Ryder."

Chapter Sixteen

Ryder's mouth hung open. He barely managed to close it before drool poured out. A bedroom sounded good, but the chamber they showed him to was a luxury suite the likes of which he'd heard of, but until that moment, hadn't believed truly existed. Whoever decorated the room clearly didn't have to worry about sticking to a budget.

Michael tossed some clothes on the bed, their weight slightly indenting the spot they landed on.

A soft mattress!

He'd slept on plenty of things, but a four-poster, king-sized bed wasn't one of them. His hand shook, reaching out to touch the cool velvet cover of the down duvet.

"If you need anything else... wait till morning," Michael ordered. "Try to stay put. I don't feel like hunting you down and hurting you." He offered a sly smile. "Gabby only said I had to keep you alive."

"Sure thing," Ryder replied. He watched the door close before the palm of his hand made contact with his forehead. He had thrown his chances with Gabrielle out the window. Not that he had many in the first place, but hope was better than nothing.

"Stupid!" His foot connected with a metal chest placed conveniently on the floor at the end of the bed. "Ow!"

It was sturdier than it looked. He bit down on his bottom lip, hopping on one foot. It was a few minutes before the pain subsided enough to put pressure on it again. Even then it was only with the help of a few well-chosen swear words.

Ryder fell back onto the bed, bouncing once before sinking in. The mattress had more spring to it than he originally thought. That didn't make it any less comfortable. His legs hung off the side, bent at the knee. Not even burying his face in a fluffy pillow could take away the anger he felt from his own slip of the tongue.

He'd put his foot in his mouth, once again. Trying to re-explain his relationship with Amy now would look like a pathetic attempt to backpedal. Being a player was one reputation he didn't have and didn't want to end up with. Why had he even thought of Amy in the first place?

Dante!

That guy could be the single reason lawyers had a bad name: a pure sleazeball through and through. He'd never spoken to the man, but Amy was quite fond of him. What a coincidence, Dante turned out to be the leader of a bunch of demons who wanted him dead.

Ryder jolted upright. "Wait a minute. It isn't a coincidence at all. Dante took Amy as a client because she was my next door neighbour." He closed his eyes, his head shaking. How had he missed that?

If it was true, Amy was in real danger. If anything happened to her, it would be his fault. As much as he felt for Gabrielle, she wasn't a constant in his life. They'd only just met. Odds were he would serve his usefulness to her and then he would be dropped off like a bag of garbage on trash day - plopped right back on his doorstep from where he would be expected to quietly return to his pathetic life and forget everything that had happened in the past day.

Amy was as close to a family as he had. Maybe he was being selfish, but if things were going back to the way they were before, he needed Amy to carry on. If something happened to her, he'd truly be alone.

Chapter Seventeen

"You going to tell me what you are thinking?" Michael asked. "You haven't moved in a while."

"How long have you been standing there?" Gabby mumbled.

"Since I took those two to their rooms," Michael replied. He inhaled deeply, huffing the air back out in a sigh. "You want to talk about it? I can lend an ear."

Gabby shook her head. "You know I don't like to say things before I know them to be true."

"I know," Michael said, turning a chair around and straddling it, "but sometimes two heads are better than one."

Gabrielle cradled her forehead between her thumb and forefinger, glancing down at the scrap of paper.

"You don't always have to prove yourself," Michael suggested. "You are perfect the way you are."

"The world doesn't think so," Gabrielle whispered.

"Men were made to have faults," Michael replied. "That way, they were more easily controlled. Don't take their shortcomings as an excuse to hide in these books. We are a team. We always have been and always will be."

"Then why don't we ever work together?" Gabby asked. "Why do the four of us split up and go our separate ways?"

"You want the truth?" Michael asked.

Gabrielle nodded.

"I think we became a little too self-absorbed," Michael admitted. "We bested everything that was thrown at us. Then there was a big gap in which nothing really happened. To put it plainly, we became too cocky. I know I did." He fired off a wink and a smile.

His sister sniffled a laugh, wiping her nose with her sleeve. "We all did," she agreed.

"That doesn't mean it has to stay that way," Michael offered. "Let me help you. I have been known to come up with a good idea once in a while."

"Okay," Gabby agreed. "I was thinking that if all four of the keys were people, they each might take on an ability based on Ihenna's favourite things."

"So," Michael continued, "flowers, writings, art, and music. Those were the things she adored more than anything else. That makes sense, in a way."

"From Ryder's translation of these scribblings, I believe it is a sonnet of some sort - perhaps a love poem written for Ihenna herself. We only have part, so it is hard to tell." Gabrielle licked her lips. "It might actually be written in the language of the gods. I know we said that before, but why is this the first time we've seen it?"

"You think Nakamire wrote it?" Michael asked.

"It crossed my mind," Gabby admitted. "Without the rest of the pieces, we can't be certain."

"Anything else?" Michael asked, one eyebrow arched.

"Yeah," Gabby relied. "Watching you and Tara, I thought maybe the four keys... the four individuals, might match with the four of us."

"They would be our mates," Michael stated. "But then Ryder mentioned he had a girlfriend earlier."

Gabrielle pursed her lips together and nodded. "I know it sounds silly. I barely know him, but..."

"You like him," Michael said, a sly grin creeping over his lips. "I'm no expert on dating, but I did my share of meaningless flings before I met Tara. Very few people sit around waiting for a soulmate to magically appear. It's in all our natures to seek out companionship. A girlfriend isn't a mate. It is merely two people taking a chance on finding one."

"That doesn't change the fact that he has one," Gabrielle argued. "I don't want to come between them. Maybe they are really happy. It is possible I am wrong and reading something into the situation that doesn't exist."

Michael sighed. "If the two of you are meant to be together, it will happen regardless of how many girlfriends he currently has. None of them will matter, because none of them will be the one woman he truly loves. Trust me, I know how it feels... now."

Gabrielle chuckled. "Who'd have thought I'd be taking advice on matters of the heart from you?"

"I don't know," Tara said, walking in. "I think he's getting the hang of being one half of a couple."

Michael took Tara's outstretched hand. "Hey," he said. "What are you doing up? I thought you were out the second your head hit the pillow."

"I was. I heard the front door close and wanted to make sure you hadn't ditched me," Tara joked.

"The front door?" Gabrielle repeated. "If we're all here, why did the door close?"

"Maybe one of your other brothers came home?" Tara suggested.

"Trust me, you'd know if they had," Michael replied. "Neither one of them knows how to be stealthy."

"That means..."

"Ryder!" Gabrielle exclaimed, bolting for the door.

Chapter Eighteen

"Running away isn't going to help," Gabby called out. A fifteen-minute lead wasn't enough to stop her from catching up.

"I'm going home," Ryder stated, his pace quickening. "You aren't going to stop me."

"I get it," Gabby replied, swallowing the lump reforming in her throat. "You love your girlfriend and don't want anything to happen to her."

"No, you don't understand!" Ryder yelled, stopping. "You can't. You have people who love you and are there for you. You have a family. I never had any of that. Amy might not be my soulmate, but she is the closest thing to family I have. The two of us for years now have only had each other to rely on. I don't expect you to understand how that feels." He threw his arms in the air, letting them fall back down at his sides.

"We're more alike than you know," Gabby argued, catching up. She gulped back - this time it was pride that was lodged in her throat. "I might even be a bit worse. I pushed away everyone close to me and have spent the better part of centuries locked away from the world. Time passed by and all I managed to do was sit and stew, constantly worried about how unfairly the world had always treated me. Truth be told, it wasn't everyone else who was judging my actions harshly, it was me. I never saw it until now - until I met you."

"Why?" Ryder asked. "Everything about you is perfect. You are strong, beautiful, and smart. I admire you for all of that."

"I always felt the need to be better than my brothers," Gabby explained. "I needed to prove I belonged, that I was an important part to the team."

The dam Gabrielle had erected long ago began to crumble. A flood of emotions burst through. Her body trembled, fearing the strange sensations it had all but forgotten.

"Sh," Ryder whispered, pulling her close. His hand stroked the back of her head. He'd done the same for Amy in the past, but never with the same passion as the woman in his arms enticed inside him. Gabrielle had lit a fire that even the strongest storm could never extinguish. He would weather the gates of hell for her if the need arose.

Gabrielle sniffled back, chuckling. "Guess it's your turn to *sh* me. I'm sorry..."

"It's okay," Ryder said, drying a few stray tears from her cheeks. As different as they were, a part them was the same. That was the part that connected them, forming a bond as strong as blood. "I need you to understand. I can't leave her alone to face Dante. It's my fault he's hanging around her in the first place."

"Okay." Gabrielle nodded. "But I am coming with you. If Dante is lurking about, you'll need my help. Lead the way."

"Actually," Ryder said, pointing across the street at a low-rise apartment complex less than a block away, "we are almost there." Forming an arch out of his eyebrows, he flashed a toothy grin before jogging to the other sidewalk.

Space was something everyone needed. Ryder was no different. Gabrielle stayed back a few paces. Normally, if there was any demonic activity in an area there would be signs. But here, now, even the tiny hairs that had alerted her to danger for centuries, remained still - no doubt suffering from an emotional overload. That left her no choice, but to rely on her other senses to sniff out potential threats.

Ryder came to a full stop. "No," he mumbled, staring at the yellow caution tape sealing off the area. "We're too late."

Gabrielle patted his shoulder. Giving emotional support wasn't her strong suit - a lack of interaction with others did that to a person.

"You don't know for sure what happened," she suggested. "Amy might be injured. We can check the hospitals if you like. Just because a crime has been committed, doesn't mean it has to be murder."

Ryder shook his head, taking a seat on the curb. "I don't know how," he said, "but I know she's gone." An emptiness travelled through his body. He'd felt it before, only once, the same night his parents were killed. Death itself used his icy grip to reach deep inside Ryder's soul, plucking out a part of him to bury along with the deceased when the time came.

A black car pulled up beside them before anything else could be said. "Get in," Merv ordered. "I've been searching for you for hours. It isn't safe for you to be sitting there. People are looking for you."

"Amy?" Ryder muttered.

"She's dead," Merv answered. "I'll explain everything on the way to a safehouse. We need to go, now!"

Chapter Nineteen

Merv glanced over his shoulder at his two new passengers. "Who is this? What did I tell you about changing your friends?"

"I thought you needed to move fast," Gabrielle replied with a scowl. "We'll explain everything on the way."

Merv's tongue pressed on the inside of his cheek. "Huh!" he said, turning his attention back to the road. "So start talking."

"You first," Ryder demanded. "What happened to Amy?"

"At first it was ruled an overdose," Merv said.

"And now?" Ryder asked.

"Now," Merv replied, eyeing the two in his rear view mirror, "they suspect foul play."

"You mean murder," Ryder mumbled.

"Yes, and I am sure I don't need to tell you who is at the top of the suspect list," Merv continued. "Someone laced her drugs with some serious chemicals. Whoever it was wanted her dead fast. It seems they got what they wanted."

"Why aren't you turning me in?" Ryder asked.

"Because it is his job to keep you safe," Gabrielle stated. "A job which he hasn't been doing very well, I might add."

"And you are?" Merv asked, his eyes nothing more than slits staring at her in the mirror.

"I'm Gabrielle," She announced.

The car tires squealed, unhappy about being forced to come to a halt quickly. He threw the gear into park. Had there been a car behind them, it would have rammed right into the bumper. Luckily, the road they were on was deserted.

"*The* Gabrielle," Merv asked.

"The one and only," Gabrielle replied, her eyebrows arched. "You were tasked with protecting the bloodline, were you not?"

"I was," Merv answered, nodding. His blank expression rivaled the look of any poker player at a high-stakes game.

"So what happened?" Gabrielle pried.

"I'll explain everything once we arrive," Merv stated, putting the car back into drive. Dust flew up from the tires as they began their rotations, spitting gravel out behind them. "It isn't too much further."

"Where are we?" Ryder asked. "I don't recognize this road."

"It wouldn't be a secret place if everyone knew where it was," Merv replied. "There is an old mine up ahead. We'll be safe there - at least for a little while. Hopefully, we can come up with a plan. I don't think it is a good idea to leave this to the courts. There is only so much we can sweep under the rug."

"I agree," Gabrielle said. "Especially with the murder of the prosecutor the other day. I'm sure your contacts are leery about being blamed with Dante's failure."

"Dante," Merv repeated. "Who is that?"

"Amy's lawyer," Ryder explained.

"Amy's lawyer killed the prosecutor?" Merv questioned. "That's taking being a sore loser to a new level."

"You have no idea what's going on, do you?" Gabrielle questioned. "For a protector, that isn't a good thing."

Merv pursed his lips together, inhaling deeply. "I suppose I don't," he admitted. "Up until the past few days, I didn't believe any of the family teachings to actually be true. None of us did."

"So why go along with it all?" Gabrielle asked.

"The position came with certain benefits," Merv replied. "We're here." He nodded at the dark entrance leading into the side of a mountain - a set of old tracks their welcome mat.

The mine's mouth loomed over them, daring them and anything else to enter. Once inside, they'd be at its mercy. With rocks overhead and below, a simple landslide could have spelled disaster, encasing them in a naturally formed crypt that no one would know to come visit.

The first couple of hundred yards were the easiest, still being under the influence of the outside light and air. The path jutted to the left, leading them to a claustrophobic's worst nightmare. The air thickened, stale and foul, as fast as the light thinned, swallowing them whole in a sea of darkness.

Gabrielle reached out, grasping at Ryder's hand. "We need to stay together," she directed. "We could easily get lost in some of the tunnels that run through here."

She hadn't been to that specific abandoned mine before, but there had been enough similar places in her past to know what to expect. This particular one had been mined dry. There were no sparkling crystals left in the wall. They would have danced before them, with or without a light source, if they existed. Whoever first found the treasure this mountain had hidden for centuries, made sure they took every bit of value out before abandoning it to sit and rot.

She scuffed her feet, finding secure footings before moving - a slow process, but worth it if they avoided wiping out, even if it did mean Merv took a large lead. The sound of pebbles, skittering about in the distance, was the guide, directing her through every twist and turn.

"We should have brought a flashlight," Ryder stated. "I'm surprised Merv didn't have one. He's usually prepared for anything."

Gabrielle bit her lip. "Oh, no," she muttered.

It felt no more uncomfortable than a mosquito bite, but that sharp prick was something much worse. She inhaled deeply, fighting the spinning feeling to no avail. Her legs buckled, sending her falling to the ground. Someone was calling her name, but they sounded far away. Her vision blurred with light, then darkness.

Chapter Twenty

Gabby's eyes opened, but refused to focus. Her arms tugged on the restraints binding them. With laboured breath, she tried again with the same result. Whatever was holding her down, it wasn't budging.

"I can hear your heart, Merv," Gabby said. "You betrayed us. That was a big mistake. You know you'll pay dearly for this in the end."

"It was a mistake I had to make," Merv admitted. "They have my family. What else could I do?"

"Your family swore an oath," Gabby argued. "You betrayed your own lineage." She shook her head, trying to alleviate the lingering fuzziness that had been inflicted on her. Her tongue darted out, but had no moisture to aid dry lips. It banged against the roof of her mouth, trying to generate some saliva.

"Isn't that ironic," Mirabelle said, waltzing in. "Do you like it?" She spun in a circle, twirling her pink gown accentuated by white elbow-length gloves that aided in the blowing of kisses to each of them. "I think it's perfect. You would be amazed at what this place has to offer a girl. It is like having a giant walk-in closet at my fingertips." She giggled.

"Mirabelle!" Merv exclaimed. "Untie me!"

"Why would I want to do that?" Mirabelle asked. "Dante wouldn't be happy with me if I did."

"I don't understand," Merv complained. "You said they were holding you captive. Where is your mother?"

"Your wife is in the next room," she scoffed. "That's right. I know all about what happened: about me; about him; about the fire that killed our real parents."

"Mirabelle, please," Merv begged. "Untie me. I am your father. I raised you. I love you."

"Perhaps at first. Then you decided he was more important!" Mirabelle yelled, pointing a single finger at Ryder. "You and your wife with all those ridiculous rules. You tried to ruin my life, and for what? A pipsqueak like him. Well, it looks like I am getting the last laugh now, aren't I?"

Spit flew through the air, landing on Ryder's face. "Yuck!" he exclaimed. "I have nothing to do with this."

"Nothing?!" Mirabelle yelled. "Nothing?! You are the reason for all of this. They regretted choosing me over you."

"Never once," Merv protested. "Your mother and I love you very much. You are our daughter."

"All you did was yell at me," Mirabelle snarled, her teeth grinding. "Now, that's all about to change."

"Please, Mirabelle," Merv begged. "Come back. We can work through this like a family."

"I have a new family now," Mirabelle said, giggling. "They give me expensive gifts and love me. Ta-ta for now, but I'll be back. I have to check on mommy dearest."

Stone scraped on stone behind them. The only door, no doubt made from the same materials and in the same drab grey colour as the rest of the room.

Gabrielle glanced around, her equilibrium returning. She struggled against the metal bindings around her arms and legs. Normally, she'd be able to easily break any substance that bound her. This was different: it was new.

"Let me see if I have this whole story right," she said in between straining grunts. "You were born into this lineage, but didn't believe the stories about your sacred vows. There were advantages if you went along with it all, though. The position meant you had money, status, and a good life."

Merv sighed, his head hanging down. "Yeah. That's about right."

"Then two other members of your order, the ones blessed with the child of the bloodline, were killed in a fire," Gabby said, continuing her struggle. "And you didn't see anything out of the ordinary about the accident?"

"It was a fire," Merv argued, shaking his head. "Fires happen. Granted it was a big one, encompassing several homes." He licked his lips. "There were reports that said it was a gas leak. I had no reason to doubt them."

"Because we all know reports are never fake," Ryder said, the corners of his lips pointing down.

"So," Gabby continued, "only two children survived. Instead of taking care of the child from the bloodline, you adopted a mortal girl? Why?"

"We talked it over with the others that remained faithful," Merv explained. "If there was actually any truth to the stories, we'd be putting ourselves in danger adopting him."

Gabby smacked her lips, shaking her head. "And he was better off being shoved from home to home, jail cell to jail cell?"

"We moved him frequently," Merv replied. "We made sure the paper trails were well buried. No one was supposed to find him. Everyone was better off that way."

"You were better off that way," Gabrielle complained. "You didn't think about Ryder's well-being. You thought about yourselves. You said you didn't believe any of it, and yet when it came to your own lives, you weren't willing to take the risk it might all be true."

"I made sure he was taken care of!" Merv yelled back. "I kept him out of jail whenever possible."

"If I could clap, I would," Ryder said. "Thank you for taking such great care of me. I hate to state the obvious, but if you hid me so well, why are we here?"

"I don't know," Merv admitted. "They shouldn't have been able to trace you."

"Actually," Dante said, strolling in, "we never lost sight of him. I hope you don't mind the interruption, but I am your host. It would be rude of me not to say... hello."

"Dante," Gabrielle said.

"I have to admit," Dante replied. "I am surprised to see you here. It's a good surprise, though. I am genuinely happy to see you. I take it the bindings are holding?"

"For the moment," Gabrielle snarled.

"Good to hear," Dante said. "Your brother found it a little too easy to break out of the last batch. Our scientists weren't happy about having to go back to the drawing board, but I think you'll find this material completely unbreakable."

"How wonderful for you," Gabby argued, straining harder against the restraints.

"You'll only hurt yourself if you keep that up," Dante suggested. "It won't break."

"Why?" Gabrielle asked. "Because I'm a woman?"

"Heavens no," Dante replied, chuckling. "My dear, I have always considered you the smartest, strongest, and most fearless of the horsemen. Not to mention, you are probably the most dangerous as well."

"Glad we agree on something," Gabrielle cursed. "You'll forgive me if I don't give up quite yet."

"Suit yourself," Dante answered. "I suppose you wouldn't be our Gabby if you didn't have the need to prove yourself a step and a half above the rest."

"She's not your anything," Ryder blurted out.

"How rude of me," Dante said, flashing a toothy grin. "I haven't introduced myself."

"I know who you are," Ryder scoffed. "You killed Amy."

"Amy?" Dante howled a rich, deep laugh. "You are worried about that little wench? You know, she sold you out for a quick fix."

"I don't believe you," Ryder argued. "Amy was my friend. She would never have done anything to hurt me."

"Never say never. With friends like that, my boy, you are better off with your enemies," Dante stated. "She set you up to take the fall for that little vandalism stunt. That pathetic prosecutor was supposed to ensure you were delivered into the hands of my colleagues at the mental institution."

Two legs of a chair scraped against the ground. Dante tossed it in front of them before straddling it.

"You'll ruin your fancy suit sitting like that," Gabrielle said, glaring.

"I have plenty more," Dante explained. "I have anything a man could ask for and more... much more."

"What about my daughter?" Merv asked, his head held down. "You sick pervert."

"Please," Dante said, holding up a hand. "I haven't touched the girl, nor do I plan to. I have no interest in her. She served a purpose: rounding the lot of you up. She'll be compensated well for her contribution to the cause."

"And my wife?" Merv snarled. "What have you done with her?"

Dante glanced around the room. "I thought someone was missing. I honestly have no idea why she isn't in here with the lot of you." He motioned with one hand. "Luke, let's reunite the family."

Chapter Twenty-One

Dante pulled a cigar from the inside pocket of his suit jacket. Pulling it under his nose, he inhaled deeply, admiration reflected in his eyes.

"You don't mind, do you?" Dante asked, a cigar cutter already clamping down on the end. Once between his lips, he drew in through it, making sure it had been properly rolled. If it had been too tight, it would have landed on the floor to be swept up as garbage.

"I always said you were raised in a gentleman's club," Gabrielle muttered.

Dante raised one eyebrow, smiling. His attention was focused on the toasting of his cigar, a ritual all smokers knew and performed. Holding the cigar at a forty-five degree angle, he gently rotated it as he allowed the flame to flicker directly underneath.

"The trick to toasting," Dante explained, "is to never let the flame directly touch the tobacco. If you do, you could char the wrapper. That would be a waste."

A whiff of smoke floated up from the end. Dante placed the cigar between his lips, gently puffing as he continued to rotate the tip over the flame until the entire end was glowing.

"Now all we need is an even burn," he said, blowing smoke over the ash of the cigar and inspecting it.

"Aren't you worried the ashes will fall all over you and make a mess?" Ryder asked.

Dante howled a deep laugh. "Long ashes that don't fall are the sign of a well-made cigar. A true connoisseur enjoys flaunting such perfection. Only amateurs have a need to flick ashes like some cheaply home-rolled cigarette."

"Sorry," Ryder snapped, rolling his eyes. "I haven't brushed up on the guide to properly smoking a cigar. It never interested me. I find inhaling smoke deeply makes me choke."

"It would," Dante agreed. "A fine cigar is never inhaled deeply, as you put it. It is as delicate to the palate as a fine wine. Meant to be sipped, not gulped."

"I'll keep that in mind next time someone offers me one," Ryder joked. "You never know when your tutelage might come in handy. Really, you may have missed your calling. Have you ever thought about teaching?"

"Unfortunately," Dante replied, chuckling, "I don't think the time will ever come when you might put my lessons to use." He looked past his captives at the stone door grinding open. "Mirabelle, I wasn't expecting Luke to bring you." He glanced at Luke who merely shrugged his shoulders.

Mirabelle pranced in. "Dante!" she exclaimed. "Things are going wonderfully."

"Things?" Dante echoed, arching an eyebrow.

"Yes," Mirabelle replied, pressing a golden chalice to her lips and gulping back its contents. "I brought them here for you, just as you asked. I figured out our little problem too."

"Problem?" Dante asked. "What problem?"

"Oh, you know," Mirabelle teased.

"No," Dante admitted. "I have no idea what you are talking about. How about you let me in on what it is?"

"About my age..." Mirabelle whined, shaking her head.

"My dear," Dante said. "I have absolutely no idea to what you are referring."

Mirabelle's lips turned into an upside down smile. "Always a gentleman," she said, pressing her gloved finger to her own lips, then transferring a kiss on its tip to his. "I know I am young and beautiful at the moment, but fifty years from now things will be different." She took another sip from her cup while skipping away.

"Obviously," Dante replied. "Can we get to the point?"

"I know!" Mirabelle replied. "And I have taken steps to make sure you find me attractive forever."

Dante shook his head. "What on earth are you talking about?"

"I know all about how you drink the blood of certain lineages to stop from aging," Mirabelle stated. "That's why you had me bring them here." She pointed to the bound trio. "You need a supply."

Dante's jaw dropped open. "Please tell me you haven't done anything foolish," he begged.

"Of course not," Mirabelle replied. "I only did what was needed for us so that we can be together forever. Our love, after all, is eternal."

Dante's cigar fell to the ground. He darted forward, grabbing the goblet from Mirabelle's hand, its contents sent flying. A copper scent wafted up from the brownish-red liquid pool that formed around it. "You foolish girl! You brought it upon yourself to decide this?"

"I don't understand," Mirabelle cried. "We are in love. Don't you want me to stay the same for you?"

"We are not in love," Dante scoffed, a red flush creeping over his face. "You are a child. I have no interest in you whatsoever. I never have. I offered you a new life: a chance to earn the things you so greatly desire... nothing more."

"I don't understand..."

"No, you don't!" Dante yelled. "So let me try to set you straight! Only very special direct descendants from the gods can have their life prolonged by drinking another person's blood. You are a mere mortal. There is nothing uniquely special about you in the least. In case you aren't following me, what that means is you can't stay young by ingesting blood." He spat on the ground. "How did you ever find out about that ritual anyways?" He glanced over at Luke.

"I didn't think she was crazy enough to try it," Luke said.

"We will talk about this later," Dante replied. "If it weren't for your heritage, I'd kill you on the spot. Is the woman dead?"

Luke nodded.

"I have to say," Dante said, chuckling, "I knew you had a nasty streak in you, but never thought for a moment you were a total psychopath." He grabbed Mirabelle's arm, forcing her to the door. "You've made things very difficult for me. I needed your mother alive. Tell me, do you feel even the slightest bit sick, knowing your own mother's blood fills your stomach?"

"She wasn't my mother," Mirabelle snarled. "You told me that yourself."

"She wasn't your biological mother. That is true," Dante answered. "But she did raise you. Isn't it love you are searching for? How ironic is it that the woman you murdered was one of the only people who was willing to give that to you freely." He turned to Luke. "Take her to a cell and prepare her for the ceremony. Send someone to take her father and the key as well."

"You needed her for the ceremony," Gabrielle muttered.

"Hmm?" Dante replied, running a single finger over his bottom lip. "Yes. I will have to make alternate plans now." He shook his head. "This is a pickle."

"She was your sacrifice," Gabrielle said, not speaking to anyone in particular.

Dante laughed. "Don't worry your pretty little head," he ordered. "I'll figure something out. While I'd love to invite you to the show, I'm afraid I can't. You do understand, don't you? Michael spoiled that."

"Your new friends might question your motives if something else goes wrong." Gabrielle stated. "That would be bad for you."

"You always were the smartest of the bunch," Dante said, smiling. "I can't allow any interference this time. You'll have to remain seated here until it is all over. You might want to say your goodbyes."

Gabrielle glanced at Ryder. "If you have a chance, take it," she ordered. "Run as fast as you can."

"Oh," Dante said. "He won't do that." A switchblade popped open in his hand. The blade pressed against Gabrielle's throat. "He knows you can die. You are helpless here, not even able to summon your trusted companion. I could slit your throat and let you bleed out... if I wanted to."

"Don't!" Ryder yelled. "I'll do whatever you want."

"No!" Gabrielle shrieked.

"That a good fellow," Dante smirked. "How about we go for a walk?"

Chapter Twenty-Two

Ryder rubbed his wrists. He'd been in handcuffs before, but police officers tended to allow a little slack so as not to bite into the skin. Here, no one seemed to care. They'd used a rough length of cord bound tightly and knotted. Even the slightest movement burned. The braided twine rubbed against his bare skin, leaving it raw and red. The chaffing hadn't reached the point of drawing blood, but still stung nonetheless.

He glanced behind him at the empty corridor. Even if he took Gabrielle's advice, there was nowhere to run to. He had no idea where he was and doubted stopping for directions would help.

"You aren't thinking about making a break for it, are you?" Dante asked, without looking back. "I am fond of Gabrielle. I'd hate to have to dispose of her."

"No!" Ryder replied, his head snapping forward. "I'm not going anywhere. I'm just a bit curious about this place."

"Well," Dante replied, "I can certainly tell you a bit about its history. "This was once a mining community. They dug deep and fast, stripping the mine of every ounce of value. Afterwards, jobs dried up and the whole place became a ghost town."

"Why is it so populated around here then?" Ryder asked.

"Glad you asked!" Dante replied. "My current employers... so to speak, need to maintain a certain level of secrecy, as well as a high volume of income. When real estate values plummeted in the area, they scooped up most of the land. This underground facility was built to satisfy... certain needs. It was easiest to accomplish that without anyone snooping around."

"It's an elaborate hideout," Ryder interrupted.

Dante laughed. "I suppose you could call it that. Regardless, after it was built, they began constructing communities nearby and then factories. Once there were jobs people flocked back, none the wiser as to what was hidden nearby."

"Planning ahead," Ryder mumbled, nodding.

"Always," Dante agreed.

"Why do you want to destroy the world?" Ryder asked. "I mean, you are a part of it."

"Who said I wanted to destroy it?" Dante asked. "You assume that unlocking the doors will be a bad thing."

"Hell does have a reputation for being a bad place," Ryder argued. "That is sort of a given."

"We can agree on that," Dante replied. "It is a terrible place. Consider how you'd feel if you were locked in Hell for eternity."

"I can only imagine what one must have to do to earn that fate," Ryder stated. "It would need to be something beyond evil."

"Hm," Dante huffed. "I would have thought you of all people would have had a better perception."

"What do you mean?" Ryder asked.

"How many times have you been found guilty of a crime and sentenced to some form of punishment?" Dante asked.

"Too many to count," Ryder admitted, frowning. "But you knew that. I was set up."

"Ponder this: what if you aren't the only one?" Dante questioned. "Ah! Here we are." He motioned to a side chamber, a little larger than a walk-in closet. "This fellow will get you dressed properly for the ceremony. I trust you will remember our agreement."

Ryder nodded. What choice did he have?

Chapter Twenty-Three

The stone door scraped closed. Muffled voices faded in the distance. Gabrielle had been left all alone.

Dante, as perfect as he seemed, had a major flaw. He was arrogant. It was that very arrogance that would be his downfall. Not a single guard had been left to watch her. It was assumed that the new material that confined her would continue to do its job.

Gabrielle's muscles flexed, straining against the tight bindings. Nothing happened. She inhaled deeply, preparing for another attempt. This time she bit down, her teeth grinding as she forced every bit of strength she possessed into her arms.

"Damn!" she yelled, letting frustration find its way out of her mind through her words. "There has to be a way!"

If she failed now, she let everyone down. The entire world was riding on her shoulders. Defeat simply couldn't be allowed to happen. She wasn't about to go down in history as the horseman who failed - assuming there was a history left to go down in.

Sometimes two heads are better than one.

"Michael," she whispered. "I could use your help now. Any chance you can hear me?"

Either I am going crazy or I can hear you. Michael's voice replied in her mind.

"That makes two of us," Gabrielle jested. "If this really is you, Dante has me locked up. I am not strong enough to break free."

A new type of metal? Dante has been experimenting with it. I guess he improved it since I last saw him. This is a new connection between us, I wonder how far it reaches. Michael said.

"What do you mean?" Gabrielle asked.

Close your eyes, Michael said. *I'm going to see if we can connect on a physical level as well.*

"You're going to will me your strength," Gabrielle mumbled. "Is that even possible?"

I guess we will find out. On the count of three. One. Two. Three.

"Ah!" Gabrielle screamed, pulling with everything she had. Her wrists beginning to wiggle. "Keep going!"

Clanks and clinks egged her on, pushing her will to its furthest limits. This was the ultimate test: winner-take-all. She was engaged in a race to determine a clear victor - the one who could withstand the breaking point, literally. Her will to succeed was pitted against the strength of her bindings.

With lungs full of air, she sunk every ounce of her being into the fight. The clasps gave way, flying upwards and embedding themselves in the rock of the ceiling. Gabrielle fell from the seat to her knees, coughing amidst a cloud of dirt raining down.

Whether Michael had actually been with her in spirit or not, she owed him thanks when this was over. Without his encouragement, she would have more than likely still been confined.

After dealing with the chair of oppression, making short work of the exit was an easy task. A single kick sent the stone door crashing against the opposite wall, squishing a lone guard in the process.

Gabrielle stepped over the mess, glancing left and right. A second guard charged towards her. She ducked from the reach of his sword, grabbing his arm and spinning him around.

"Where is the ceremony?" Gabrielle asked, pinning the man to a wall, his arm behind his back. "I can break it!"

"Go ahead!" the guard yelled. "Far worse would happen if I told you." The snap was barely audible over the man's howls of pain.

"I can do far worse as well," she snarled in his ear. "I could dismember you piece by piece."

The guard's breath laboured. He glanced to his left, giving her the information she needed.

"I'll take your robe," she demanded, pulling it off his shoulders. "If you move, I'll kill you."

The man winced as his broken arm withdrew from the sleeve. He spun around, dagger in hand. Gladia hissed, striking at his throat. His body slumped in a pile on the ground.

"I did warn you," Gabrielle said, pulling the hood of her new red robe over her head. "Gladia!" A snake-skin belt replaced the golden rope that was meant to be tied around the waist.

Chapter Twenty-Four

Gabrielle kept her eyes pointed down. Being recognized too early would blow the chance of any plan she might be able to come up with. A gong vibrated in an adjoining room. The rest of the cloaked figures formed a line, entering in procession to take their place. Each wanted to be as close to the altar as possible, pushing and prodding for the best seats.

Gabrielle hung back, taking in the surroundings. It was almost familiar, being exactly as Michael had described his own experience. There was something missing, though. Either her demon radar was off or the room was filled with mortal worshipers. In the end, it didn't matter much; she didn't discriminate when it came to slaughtering the enemy.

Gabrielle winced, glancing up at a swinging cage, lurking above. It dangled, waiting to be lowered. Its sole purpose was to spike the key, draining blood for the ceremony. Her eyes desperately searched the room. There was no sign of Ryder.

Elbows and shoulders nudged her along, forcing her closer to Dante than she wanted to be. Going with the flow put her in the second row on the opposite side of a deep pit. Copying the others, she bowed and knelt, waiting for the ceremony to begin.

A second, louder clang of the gong vibrated through the room. Silence swept over the crowd. Anticipation grew thick, filling any unoccupied spaces. Dante's arms opened, holding his palms up. His flock divided, like a holy parting of a sea. Two large double doors opened to a procession of banners and special cloaks, marked in gold designs.

The designs! They were written in the same odd language as the paper Ryder had found. If only she knew what they meant.

Standing at the threshold, a legion of followers marched on the spot providing a drumming tempo. The rest of the congregation joined in as the parade began. Mirabelle entered of her own accord, pulling a chain attached to her father's neck. She pulled. He stumbled. Neither one of them had learnt a thing from this experience.

Gabrielle caught her first sight of Ryder, three rows back. It took all of her self-control not to gasp at the sight of him dressed in a white tuxedo adorned with an assortment of ruby red accessories. Stunned momentarily by his beauty, she missed the beginning of the service, tuning back in too late to help Merv and his daughter escape a fiery end.

Gabrielle hadn't anticipated that move. She'd assumed Dante had needed the blood of a female in the clan. After Mirabelle murdered her mother, technically there wasn't one. Instead, he substituted father and daughter together as the next best thing.

A gasp no louder than a whisper escaped her lips - silent, but not unheard. Ryder glanced in her direction, their eyes exchanging the tiniest glimmer of hope. He nodded, turning his head back.

Two cloaked figures dragged Ryder across to the altar, tossing him on the ground. Refusing to stay down, he stood, squaring his shoulders to Dante.

"I have a plan," Ryder announced.

Dante arched his eyebrows. "Do you? Please, by all means, enlighten us."

Ryder cleared his throat. He raised both his arms in the air much as Dante had previously. "The key is only to be used when true love fails and one partner stands accused." He glanced around the room at the sea of red cloaks mocking him. "I said: the key is only to be used when true love fails and one partner stands accused."

"Yes," Dane replied. "We heard you the first time. Unfortunately, that trick won't work here." He leaned forward. "There isn't a single demon in the room."

Gabrielle shook her head. That was the worst plan she had ever heard of, and over the years, she'd been privy to some terrible ones. With the masses distracted it was, however, the opportunity she was waiting for.

"Gladia!" Gabby yelled. Her belt slithered off her midsection, forming a perfect arrow. Travelling at a speed faster than sight, her weapon took out a selection of the largest guards. Panic ensued as the not-so-loyal followers fled. Dante's plan had been almost perfect, but he hadn't anticipated the fickle nature of men. Her own plan began to come together. Hiding in plain sight from the faithful was easier than anticipated.

Those few minutes were precious, allowing her to position herself between the guards around the altar and Ryder. Gladia returned, coiled around her arm and hissing.

"Stay away," Gabby ordered, backing up with one hand latched on to Ryder's wrist.

Gladia spit at each guard as they took turns trying to move in closer for an attack. The snake hissed and lunged at the first to try, dropping him in his tracks.

"Don't let them escape," Dante ordered, heading towards a back entrance. A sequence of stones on the wall appeared, slightly pushed in from the rest. He saluted Gabrielle with two fingers before disappearing completely.

"Your leaders have left you to die," Gabby stated. "Run away now and I won't have to kill you."

The guards exchanged glances. When Dante left, he took their courage with him. Their weapons clanged together in a pile, each running for a different exit.

"We need to hurry," Gabby said. "I'm guessing there is some sort of self-destruct in place. If something down here blows, these rooms will all be buried under a tonne of rocks."

"We definitely don't want to be here when that happens," Ryder agreed.

"So either you can move fast or I'll have to carry you," Gabrielle threatened. "This isn't a time to worry about dignity."

"I pretty much don't have any left after my plan bombed," Ryder admitted. "Carry away!"

Gabrielle scooped him over her shoulders like a sack of potatoes and ran for the same door Dante had exited from. Mimicking her former friend's movements prior to disappearing, she pressed on several stones, each grinding as it moved. A secret door popped open.

"Damn!" Gabrielle exclaimed.

"What?" Ryder asked, still upside down, his face flushed.

"A dead end," Gabby answered. "There are three rooms. There must be a way out hidden in one of them."

"Put me down," Ryder ordered. "I can help look. Sometimes, two heads are better than one."

"I've heard that somewhere before," Gabrielle replied, lowering him to his feet. She took stock of the open doors: a dressing room no bigger than a closet, a library of sorts, and a gentleman's club. A quick mental calculation of the possibilities eliminated the clothes chamber, narrowing the choice to the remaining two.

"Wait!" Ryder called out.

"The end one," Gabrielle said, "it has to be the right choice. It holds everything Dante indulges in."

"That's why it isn't the right choice," Ryder argued. "It has everything he wants. We are looking for an emergency way out. I don't think he would want to escape from that room. Trust me."

Without waiting for a response, he headed to the middle room. He had seen a similar layout before, granted it had been a little less well-kept. Here, the books were neatly ordered on the shelves that lined every wall and completely dust free. His fingers ran across the spines, taking in every title, every author, before coming to rest on a faded, tan colour hardcover book.

"This is it!" he yelled, yanking the rare edition from its spot. He stepped back.

The faint squeals of grinding gears foreshadowed the future. The pair took turns watching every corner for movement. Two bookcases moved forward, opening to another corridor.

"There's a light at the end of the tunnel," Ryder said, grabbing Gabrielle's hand.

A crack louder than the bellow of a thunder clap directly overhead sent shivers down their spines. They moved as one, desperate to outrun the horror that lay behind them. Howls of pain and fear vibrated through the walls as stone and dirt poured down on the trusting fools left behind.

Dust and smoke swirled out of the entrance to the old mine shaft. The mountain itself transformed into a fiery dragon, its breath unleashed through open mouth. A great gush of flame exploded forth, seeking to destroy any who attempted escape.

Gabrielle and Ryder leapt. Their bodies flew through the air, landing twenty feet away. Both laid face-down, limp and singed.

Chapter Twenty-Five

"Are you hurt?" Gabrielle asked, using her hands to wave dust out of her face. Taking a once-over, she was satisfied her own injuries were already beginning to heal. Once home, they would quickly disappear completely.

Ryder coughed. "Bruised and battered, but I'll live." He stood, watching rocks as they slid down the mountainside. "They buried their own people."

Pillows of smoke wafted upwards, the fire below extinguished by the very landslide it had created. The beast's belly rumbled one last time, before boulders shut its mouth permanently. In centuries, a team of scientists would chip away at the stone and uncover the greatest scientific find of the ages. Until then, secrets were safe.

"Yeah," Gabrielle answered, picking up the book that had saved them and dusting it off. "I think we were the intended targets of all of that. How did you know it was that room? This book?"

"A hunch at first," Ryder admitted. "Then I saw the book. I knew it didn't belong there. It should have been at the library. That book is the one my mother always read to me. It must have been taken at some point and transferred to that room."

"Why would Dante make this the lever? It's a rather large coincidence." Hand outstretched, she offered the edition to him.

"Thank you," Ryder replied, pulling her close. "Maybe some things are simply meant to be. Do we need to question every gift we are given?" His free hand caressed her cheek, brushing a few stray strands off her face, before cupping her chin. His lips pressed against hers.

The smacking of hands clapping together destroyed the moment before it fully had a chance to bloom. Their first kiss was shattered by reality.

"Dante!" Gabby exclaimed, squaring her shoulders to her old friend while keeping Ryder behind her.

"Yes," Dante replied. "Oh, don't worry. I graciously accept being bested by the most deadly and beautiful of the horsemen."

"Why are you doing this?" Gabby asked, eyeing the man's movements carefully. Vicious predators circled their prey before making a final attack in the same manner he now stalked them.

"I thought you of all people would have figured it out," Dante mused, his lips curling into a mischievous grin.

"If this is about what happened on the mountain," Gabby said, "I am the only one to blame. I made the mistakes."

Dante howled a bone-chilling laugh. "It's funny how we each remember the events of that day differently, isn't it? Here you are ready to be the martyr and sacrifice yourself."

"I rushed things," Gabby stated, biting her lip. "I took on too many at once. I jeopardized the fight."

"Are you telling me you couldn't handle it?" Dante asked. He glanced at her face from one side and then the other. "I didn't think so. No, Gabrielle, I believe you were as capable then as you are now. What happened that day was not a result of your doing."

Gabby's tongue peeked out of the corner of her mouth. "You can't blame Michael for what happened. He was only trying to protect me."

"Tsk tsk," Dante said, waving a finger. "You are jumping to conclusions. Just because Michael feels he is the centre of the world, doesn't make it true."

"If not Michael, then who?" Gabby yelled. "Why do you want to destroy the world?"

Dante smiled. "So dramatic," he mocked. "Have you been taking lessons from your brothers? Ah well, the answer is for me to know, and one day, you to figure out."

"Are you simply letting us go?" Gabby questioned.

"Yes," Dante replied, chuckling. "I already conceded loss. The horsemen take this round. That's two keys for you."

"And that doesn't bother you?" Gabby asked.

"Not at all," Dante answered. "There are still two more to find. The odds are good I'll end up with at least one, don't you think? Send my regards to your brothers."

"Dante!" Gabby called out. "What's the endgame?"

"Endgame?" Dante echoed. "If it is in fact a game, what fun would it be to tell you?" He shoved his hands in his pant pockets, turning to leave. His lips puckered, whistling a daunting tune she'd heard only once before, but couldn't remember from where.

"You know we have a duty to stop you!" Gabby yelled after him. "We will do everything in our power to make sure we do."

"I'm counting on it," Dante said, chuckling. "You each are cursed with a sense of duty to protect that which our fathers created. How fitting, a planet born out of love shall be destroyed by it. Until we meet again..."

Gabby watched Dante stroll away, shadows leaving nothing but a silhouette in the distance as if they had been paid the highest price to conceal his existence.

"What do we do now?" Ryder asked, placing his hands on her hips.

"We go home," Gabby replied, her lips grazing against his. "My brothers need to know what has happened. Then we'll make a plan."

"And Dante?" Ryder asked. "He's not going away... not completely. How do we prepare?"

"I don't know," Gabby answered. "I guess there are some things we have no control over. We'll figure it out... together."

"Who are you?" Ryder asked. "And what have you done with Gabrielle?"

Gabby giggled. "This is the new improved me," she explained. "If I've learned anything over the past couple of days, it's that if we are to succeed, we need to work as a team."

"I like the new you," Ryder admitted. "I think we can look forward to a long and happy partnership."

"Shall we?" Gabby asked.

"Lead the way, my lady," Ryder replied. "Wherever you go, I'll follow."

Gabby glanced back over her shoulder. *Until we meet again, Dante, may the gods' grace shine down on you.*

THE END

Author's Message

I hope you enjoyed reading Gabrielle and Ryder's story as much as I did writing it. Be sure to watch social media or my website for more Four Horsemen Novels coming soon.

Flower Shields: Michael's story

Drawing Strength from Words: Gabrielle's Story

Hitting the High Note: Uriel's Story (Coming Soon)

When the Paint Dries: Raphael's Story (Coming Soon)

Thank you for reading! If you enjoyed this book, please browse through some on my other titles currently available.

ABOUT THE AUTHOR

C.A. King is the recipient of several awards, including: The Hamilton Spectator Readers' Choice Award for 2017 Best Author; The Brant News Readers' Choice Award for 2017 Best Author; Readers' Favourite award in the short story/novella category; the 2017 SIBA Award for Best New Adult; and the 2017 SIBA Award for Best Novella.

Currently residing in Brantford, Ontario Canada, she lives with her two sons. She began her writing career after the tragic loss of her parents and husband. Redirecting her emotions through writing became therapeutic in her battle with depression and in 2014 she decided to publish some of her works.

Other Titles from C.A. King

The Portal Prophecies

These great titles in C.A. King's The Portal Prophecies series are available now at most online book retailers:

A Keeper's Destiny

A Halloween's Curse

Frost Bitten

Sleeping Sands

Deadly Perceptions

Finding Balance

Volume I (Books 1-3)

Volume II (Books 4-6)

The prophecies are the key to their survival. Can they solve them in time?

Shattering the Effects of Time

Join the Shinning brothers, Jessie, Dezi and Pete as they set out on a quest to save their younger sister. No magic known to them or their friends has ever been able to reverse the grip of time. A few legends, however, exist mentioning ancient items that may hold the key to do exactly that.

This brand new series will take you on a search for the Fountain of Youth and Mermaids; a quest for the Holy Grail; a trip to visit Daryl the mountain guru, in the hunt for the Cinamani Stone; on a search for Ambrosia, the food of the Gods; and other adventures.

Surviving the Sins: Answering the Call

The prophecies are being rewritten. This time someone is using the seven deadly sins: Lust; Gluttony; Greed; Sloth; Wrath; Envy; and Pride, to unlock an ancient evil. The book falls into Jade's hands to answer destiny's call. Can she survive the sins?

Surviving the Sins: Pride

No one is safe when a witch's pride is at stake.

Prudance is back in Pewterclaw, and she isn't about to give up her prestigious status without a fight - especially not because of vampires. As an eighth-generation witch, she plans to do whatever it takes to stop the proposed new legislation from becoming law, including waking the dead for help.

Humility isn't in her vocabulary. With an ego spinning out of control and ancestral power at her fingertips, Prudance weaves a plot to keep Jade and Gavin separated. Will it be enough to satisfy the spirits she summoned?

When her pride costs more than she bargained for, someone has to pay the tab - but who will it be?

Surviving the Sins: Lust

What Mother doesn't know won't hurt her.

Lucinda has spent her entire existence running The Organization and looking after Mother's needs without complaint. That's about to change. A burning desire had manifested inside her - one she could no longer deny... Lust.

When Constable Safron Black shows up unexpected with news of an imprisoned God, Lucinda unravels. With power fuelling her passion, she'll do anything to make Morynx her mate.

****

Jade and her friends find themselves at a standstill. They have already failed to stop Pride from completing its task and they haven't located any victims for the other six sins. A strange fire in the municipal office puts them hot on the trail of what could be answers. Will they be in time to stop the dial from moving and further opening the way for Morynx?

When Leaves Fall: A Different Point of View Story

Ralph wakes up to what others only experience in a nightmare. Chained to a shed, he has no idea where he is, or who his captor is. His memories a blurred at best. As the days press on he finds himself experiencing a roller coaster of feelings. Hunger, thirst and pain become his only companions. Flashbacks of a happier time are all he has to keep him going. As his situation deteriorates, he finds himself doubting the very things he wants most - a family.

When Leaves Fall is a dramatic-thriller with a twist. Keep the tissue box close for the ending.

Tomoiya's Story

A Vampire Tale. She had a secret but she wasn't the only one who had something to hide.

Book I ~ Escape to Darkness

Book II ~ Collection Tears

Book III~ Coming Soon

Peach Coloured Daisies: A Cursed by the Gods Story

He couldn't die. An ancient curse meant she always did. This time, that was going to change - one way or another.

When Daisy's grandmother, her last living relative, passes away, she doesn't know where to turn. Things go from bad to worse when a local psychic tells her about a curse. Alone and confused, she ends up in front of her college professor's office, ready to cry her heart out in his arms.

Matt Demi might be the son of a God, but he's living the life of a cursed man. He's had to watch the woman he loves die on her twenty-first birthday countless times. Nothing he does seems to be able to affect the outcome. When she shows up at his office scared out of her wits by a psychic's prediction, he vows this time will be different.

With only three days, Matt will need to embrace a side of him he swore off long ago to save her, but will he lose himself in the process?

Flower Shields: A Four Horsemen Novel

Meet the four horsemen: Michael, Gabrielle, Uriel and Raphael. For centuries their job has been to guard the gates of hell, making sure they never open. Without the keys, there was never any real threat. That's about to change. There are rumours on the horizon that demon followers unearthed scrolls that explain exactly how to find the lost keys. This new battle is a race to see which side locates them first.

Michael couldn't care less about the love story behind how and why the world was created. In fact, nothing matters to him other than keeping the gates to hell closed. If one of the lost keys ever fell into the wrong hands, all humanity would be doomed. He's not going to let that happen - at any cost.

****

Tara's life is nothing short of a disaster. She's managed to flunk out of college with about the same amount of dignity as every relationship she's been in. The only constant in her life has been her love for flowers. When she's attacked at work, a stranger comes to her aid. Michael might be good-looking, but he's also arrogant, bossy and crazy. He's also her only chance to figure out who attacked her and why. Should she follow her heart and trust him - or listen to her head and run?

Miracles Not Included

A heartfelt romantic story about: life; love; loss; and learning to love again. If only life came with instructions and a warning label ~ Miracles Not Included.

****

Chris was born to be a writer. Even the smallest of details couldn't pass without notice, often becoming part of a plot for her next novel. The one thing she never saw coming was her husband's sudden illness.

Jason loved his wife from the moment they met. Nothing could ever change that - nothing except the death sentence he'd been handed - a terminal cancer diagnosis.

His story was ending: Hers was starting a new chapter and more than one miracle was needed to turn the page.

Twisted Tales of a Dead End Street

A paranormal mystery laced with comedic undertones: Twisted Tales of a Dead End Street.

Nine neighbours were invited to the mysterious dinner party at 9 Nine Street. Their host, the owner of the mansion, had more planned for the evening than just roast beef.

When the secret of their quiet street was revealed, everything changed, blurring the lines between the tangible and the paranormal.

Was the number nine the difference between life and death? Would any of them survive long enough to uncover the truth? They would each soon find out this wasn't a simple case of who-done-it so much as one of what was being done and by whom.

Shot Through The Heart: A Faerie Tale

A tale of two worlds - one filled with magic; the other void of it. But what happened to those trapped between the two? Adelia was about to find out...

Magic and structure were the foundations of her existence. Temptation controlled the ability to destroy everything she knew. The world of me held a powerful allure over her heart, waking that which ad long been dormant. It enticed her, snagging her in a web of emotions.

A decision had to be made. Was feeling love for the first time worth sacrificing magic and immortality?

www.ingramcontent.com/pod-product-compliance
Lightning Source LLC
Chambersburg PA
CBHW031113260626
47172CB00001B/347